Again

Pamela Beason

WildWing Press

AGAIN is a work of fiction. Names, characters, places, and incidents are either the product of the author's imagination or are used fictitiously, and any resemblance to actual persons living or dead, business establishments, events, or locales, is entirely coincidental.

ISBN: 978-0-9983149-2-1

Published in the United States of America by:

WildWing Press
Bellingham, WA

Prologue

The moment she peered through the peephole in the front door, Gail Langston knew that tragedy had hunted her down.

Two Washington State Highway Patrol officers stood on her porch, heads down, rainwater sheeting from their plastic-shrouded caps. If it had been only one man, or even two male officers, she might not have felt the cold grip of panic clutch at her heart.

It was a gray Monday in mid-September. Her head ached, and her throat was raw with a strep infection.

She'd hung up the phone only seconds ago, after chatting with her mother in Seattle.

Her daughter Charlie was in the kitchen, making the cookies for a business network meeting they were both supposed to attend that evening.

That left Elisa, her half–Guatemalan stepdaughter, who sometimes transported trees and rolled boulders with the backhoe at Langston Green, the family-owned plant nursery.

There was also her husband, Terry, driving alone on a busy highway in the rain to make arrangements for his father's funeral.

Please God, let this pair of uniforms be collecting for charity. Toys for Tots, coats for foster kids . . .

She opened the door.

Both officers raised their faces to meet her eyes.

"Mrs. Terrence Langston?" the male officer asked.

So it was Terry. Her heart thudded once in her chest, and

then it felt like it stopped.

"Is he dead?" Although the words burned her throat, the calmness of her voice surprised her.

Her quiet question surprised the officers even more. The man's face froze, his mouth half-open as he prepared to give the speech. The female officer's eyes abruptly filled with tears, and she glanced down at the welcome mat to gather her composure.

Gail pulled the door wide and stepped back. "You may as well come in."

She tried to read their faces as they sat across from her in the easy chairs and filled in the tragic details. A man driving with a Chihuahua in his lap had lost control, plowed through the grassy median, and run head-on into Terry's car. Both vehicles were totaled. Terry's had burst into flames on impact. Only the dog had survived.

Had the dog owner been married? Did his wife at least get the Chihuahua back? Distraught, Gail bit her lip. What kind of wife—correction, widow—thought about such things at a time like this? She should be in hysterics. Instead, she felt numb. Everything seemed fuzzy and distant, as if she were observing the scene through a thick bank of fog.

Beside her on the couch, her daughter Charlie sobbed, one hand clutched to her chest, the other pressed against her open mouth. How would her other daughter, Elisa, handle this news? First, her birth mother had abandoned her, and now, her father had died.

"Would you like some tea?" she asked the officers.

They shook their heads. Sitting stiffly, wet hats in their laps, they were no doubt cold and uncomfortable. They were eager to leave. She didn't blame them. She wished she had the option of leaving.

The officers slid their business cards onto the coffee table.

She walked them to the door and watched them dash through the rain to their cruiser. They'd talk about her when they were back on the road. If they were kind, they'd say how composed and polite and gracious she had been. If they were more inclined toward harsh comments, they'd say she was cold.

She hadn't wanted to explain to them that she'd been through it all before.

Twice.

Chapter 1

Gail attributed the first quiver of her florist shop to the pounding of the pile driver at the construction site a block away. But when the light fixtures continued to sway and the doors of the refrigerated cases popped open, she knew it was an earthquake.

She'd been clearing out the cash register at the end of the day, and for a few seconds she stood immobile and breathless, holding on to the front counter like a wobbly drunk while the floor rippled beneath her feet. Then a crystal vase shimmied off a storage shelf and shattered on the floor, and she dashed to save the rest. The light fixture swung overhead as she knelt among broken glass in front of the cabinet of vases, pressing her hands against the doors to keep them closed.

Ceramic chattered against glass inside. She hoped she was not going to end up with piles of chipped and useless inventory. After taking several workshops on basic home repairs so she wouldn't feel so clueless without Terry, she knew how to replace hinges and locks and how to plane the cabinet door if it didn't hang right after this, but there was no way to make a broken vase marketable again.

Behind her, the heavy leather-bound display book of flower-arrangement photos danced off the front counter and slammed onto the tile floor with a startlingly loud clap. A slip of paper flew out from between its pages and came to rest a few yards away, sliding halfway beneath a corner of the welcome mat.

Earthquakes were a hazard of living in the Pacific Northwest, with its ring of volcanoes and shifting tectonic plates. Each quake usually lasted only a few seconds; over the years she'd experienced at least a dozen brief twitches and thunks as the region's topography shifted. The local news was always predicting that the "Big One" could hit at any time, but nothing close to a catastrophic quake had arrived in the decades she'd lived in the area.

The standard advice was to go outdoors, away from buildings, but she couldn't afford to lose any more glassware. Outside, the whooping cacophony of car alarms was abruptly punctuated by a human scream that ended in a crash of screeching metal. Gail's heart leaped into her throat.

Charlie! Elisa! How far did this earthquake extend? Her daughters were thirty miles away in Woodinville. Was Elisa safe at the Langston Green nursery? Was Charlie's florist shop still standing?

As soon as the shaking stopped, Gail grabbed the business phone on the countertop. A busy signal, predictably, followed by the message that all circuits were busy; please try again later. She retrieved the order book from the floor, pulled the slip of paper from beneath the welcome mat.

No flower is more beautiful than you.

How had she missed yet another of Terry's notes? He'd been in the habit of leaving her little messages everywhere, and she'd thought that after two years, she'd surely discovered every one. While he was alive, the handwritten slips of paper had been a source of delight. Now each one was a sharp stab to the heart.

"Oh, Terry," she murmured. "We just had an earthquake. Felt like a big one. I wish you were here to help." She tucked the piece of paper into her pocket, then pulled her cell phone out of her purse and walked outside.

The large metal sign that had graced the café next door now lay in a twisted heap on top of a mangled green Prius. The car honked loudly and continuously in distress. Observers held their hands over their ears as a portly man repeatedly thrust his key fob at the Prius. "I can't shut it off. Shit! I don't know how to shut it off!"

No bodies lay in the street; that was a relief. She didn't smell smoke or gas. Her cell phone buzzed. She pressed one hand over her ear as she answered.

"Mom!" Charlie breathed. "Are you okay? We only got a weird surfing motion here, but I heard that Seattle got the worst of the quake. What's all that noise I hear?"

They assured each other that they were unscathed, although when a woman passing by stared at Gail's leg, she realized she was bleeding onto her gray trousers. Bending over, she plucked a shard of glass from her kneecap, then pressed her hand against the small wound as she asked Charlie, "Have you heard from Elisa?"

"Nobody's answering the office phone at Langston Green, and her cell phone just goes to voicemail."

The Prius finally ceased its frantic honking. Gail listened to her own heartbeats in the tense silence that ensued, trying not to panic at her daughter's words. She checked her watch. "The nursery is closed."

"And Elisa is not exactly famous for carrying her cell phone," Charlie reminded her.

True. Her adopted daughter spent most of her time out in the acres of fields that made up the Langston Green nursery, watering rows of trees and bushes, harvesting to fill orders, replanting and repairing as needed. And she rarely remembered to tuck her cell into a pocket.

Terry had willed a three-quarter share of the nursery to Elisa, with one quarter going to Terry's business partner,

Gerald Donaldson. As her father's second-in-command, Elisa had been the natural choice to take over as the nursery manager. Although her stepdaughter wasn't sharing bad news, Gail knew things were not going well. The loss of Terry's leadership and all his business relationships with the community had hit Langston Green hard. Elisa's work hours had lengthened; the frown lines on her forehead had deepened. Elisa never asked for help. She lived at the nursery 24-7 in an apartment above the offices in the old Langston Green homestead farmhouse. Gail and Charlie rarely saw her these days. Elisa's only close friend and confidant seemed to be her cat, Simon, and he wasn't talking.

"I called Gerald," Charlie told her. "He was already home when the quake hit. He didn't know whether Elisa had plans tonight. I'll keep trying her phone and try to get over to the nursery, but traffic is gridlocked here."

Gail glanced down the street to the closest intersection. The traffic lights were out. Cars were already stacking up, with all the drivers simultaneously confused as they tried to keep track of whose turn was next through the new four-way stop. "It's going to be bad here, too, sweetheart, but I'll lock up and start home now. And I'll keep trying Elisa's phone, too."

The traffic was even worse than Gail expected because the floating bridges across Lake Washington, the two busiest east-west routes, were closed until they could be checked for structural damage. All the commuters were funneled onto the same roads that Gail normally took around the north end of the lake. Many traffic lights were out at the ends of off-ramps, backing traffic up onto the highways. Unprepared drivers ran out of gas and snarled traffic further. To make matters worse, just after dark, it started to rain.

Gail spent the time imagining horrible scenarios involving Elisa—a backhoe accident, a building collapse, a natural gas explosion—and railing at God for this latest insult. Wasn't it bad enough that Terry had been killed, that the local economy was in shambles, that the family business was sinking like the *Titanic*? Now, an earthquake? *Please God, don't take Elisa, too.* Others were far worse off. She knew she should feel guilty for this little pity party she was throwing herself in her three-year-old Lexus. Then again, she told herself, she had good reason to feel cursed.

She'd had less than a year with career soldier Keith Garrett. He had been killed while flying his army helicopter in what should have been a routine transport mission between bases stateside. The engine had seized up, the rotors had stopped turning, and helicopters did not glide.

Gail Garrett had been nineteen years old, two months pregnant, and suddenly a widow.

A car horn sounded angrily behind her, breaking into her reverie, and she pulled forward to fill the twenty feet of space that had opened in the crawling traffic. *Happy now?* She glanced in the rearview mirror at the car behind her where a bearded young man was throttling his steering wheel.

Keith, too, had been an impatient young man. She wondered what he would have grown into over time. Heck, she wondered what *she* would have grown into after years as a military wife.

For six years after the army chaplain showed up at her door, her world had been melancholy and monochromatic. The only spot of color in her life had been her daughter Charlene, whose disposition was as bright as her golden hair.

Then Charlie's first-grade teacher fell in love with the little girl's mother. Mark Branderman proposed to Gail during a field trip to the science museum. Nineteen six-year-olds had cheered when she said yes.

Less than five months later, a week before the wedding, Mark fell to his death while scaling a rock face in the North Cascades. Convincing herself that she was not a two-time widow because they hadn't actually tied the knot yet, Gail had swallowed her sorrow and dedicated herself to being a single, if lonely, mother. She was never going to get involved with a risk-taking man again. No pilots, no climbers. In fact, she'd planned never to get involved at all.

When Charlie was nine, Gail had met Terrence Langston. He'd already sown his wild oats in the Peace Corps and brought home an exotic Mayan wife, who later deserted their marriage and fled back to Guatemala, leaving him with their daughter, Elisa, also nine years old.

Terry had understood what it was like to lose a loved one. He was a hard-working, kind, charming man who had no desire to fly helicopters or scale mountains or even travel to foreign countries again. He was running the family business he'd inherited, a neighborhood nursery called Langston Green, and he had plans to expand the business into flower shops.

Everyone said the third time was the charm. So Gail dared to believe in love and to hope again, and she and Terry had a pleasant, tranquil, and prosperous life for nearly twenty-three years. They raised two very different daughters into happy, independent young women.

Then her luck had run out, and the third-time charm was over.

Since Terry's death, Gail had been coasting, slowly losing momentum with no particular goal in mind for the future. Adjusting to harsh reality had been easier when her daughter was young. She'd had to stay focused then for the sake of her child. These days, she felt like she was sleepwalking through life.

The accidental deaths of three healthy lovers simply didn't happen to normal women, at least not in peacetime. Maybe she'd already had all the luck in love she was going to get in this life. Maybe she was cursed. Or more likely, she *was* the curse.

Oh God, where could Elisa be? She pressed the hands-free button on her steering wheel and instructed the device, "Call Elisa."

"Hi, you've reached Elisa Langston. Well, not really, because I can't come to the phone right now. Leave—"

Gail clicked the system off.

The rain lessened, and she twisted the wiper control to "Intermittent." The red taillights ahead went out, and she moved her foot from the brake to the accelerator for a minute. After an hour and a half of crawling forward by what seemed like inches, she finally received an update from Charlie.

"I found Elisa. Or, actually, some guy found her at the nursery."

"Some guy? What do you mean, he found her?"

"A tree fell on her."

Gail's heart leaped into her throat. "My God! Is she okay? Is she . . . alive?"

"Don't panic, Mom. I'm at Evergreen hospital now with her. Well, not actually *with* her, because she's in surgery."

"Surgery?" Gail's hands tightened on the steering wheel.

"Take a breath, Mom. They say she'll be fine. She has a fractured leg and a concussion, and I think they said bruised ribs, too. They're setting her leg, putting in pins, but they say she'll fully recover in a few months. And you know Elisa; that means she'll be out wrestling trees again within a week."

Yes, that sounded like Elisa all right. "I'll come to the hospital as soon as I can." Gail pressed the "End Call" button.

The car in front of her took the opportunity to make a right turn onto a side road. Could that possibly be a shortcut? Not according to the GPS map on her dash. She knew no other way to get to the hospital. Her Lexus was stuck slogging through this après-quake traffic; she felt like she was running a marathon through knee-deep mud.

Elisa's being taken care of, she reminded herself. *Charlie's with her*. The two girls she and Terry had raised had grown into strong young women.

Gail made a vow to herself to help more with the nursery, whether or not Elisa invited her to. Truth be told, she'd probably enjoy working in the nursery more than creating bouquets in a flower shop. Terry had opened the flower shop and installed her in it because he'd wanted to give his wife a safe, easy, pretty job. He'd never known her as the rough military brat she'd been a decade before she met him. She'd learned to enjoy working with flowers and creating arrangements, but the work had quickly become monotonous. The huge Langston Green nursery was the center of the family business, and Gail yearned to jump into those acres of greenery. She could plant trees; she could pot plants; she could even learn to drive the backhoe.

Then again . . . no. She clutched the steering wheel tighter, reminding herself that she couldn't abandon her florist shop. She couldn't afford to hire someone to take her place there right now. When her husband was alive, both flower shops had been busy, successful showcases for the nursery and greenhouse products. Gail's Flowers now seemed like a place where Langston Green products went to wither away, shivering in their refrigerated cases. She was ashamed that she could no longer keep up her end of the family business. Terry had probably believed he was ensuring her financial security by willing her the Seattle shop, but he hadn't foreseen the future. She was hanging on to the business by her fingernails.

But she could still work at the nursery on her days off, and after business hours during the long summer days. In fact, she decided, helping at Langston Green would give her a new sense of purpose. She had a vast surplus of spare time. It was the one advantage of being a widow with nearly zero social life.

As Evergreen Hospital finally came into view, she breathed a sigh of relief. She'd survived the quake, she was out of the crawling traffic, she had a plan to make the future feel more satisfying.

Then she met Leon.

Chapter 2

Leon Maxwell would never forget when the earthquake hit Woodinville. The actual day of the quake was a blur of hyperactivity at Fire Station 11, with the engine crew racing around turning off gas from ruptured lines and squelching minor fires. In the aid truck, he and his EMT partner, Jonathan Park, had zoomed from one location to another, treating gashes and broken bones from falling bricks and snapped tree limbs and a multitude of minor car accidents.

The day after the quake was only slightly less hectic. But most important, it was the day he met Gail Langston.

Gail's daughter Elisa was his patient. On the day of the quake, a 911 call directed him and Jon to a small dark young woman trapped under a fallen tree at the Langston Green nursery. Elisa Langston had a badly broken leg, bruised ribs, and a concussion, and she'd been laying there for hours in the cool evening rain. She was by far the most interesting rescue of the day, hypothermic and raving about an angel who had appeared to save her.

The following day, after he and Jon delivered a patient to the hospital, they took a break from the buzz of activity to check on Elisa. Her mother and her sister were in her room. At the first glimpse of Gail, Leon felt an unusual surge of attraction.

He tried to stay in professional mode in that hospital room. Jon, on the other hand, went instantly and embarrassingly gaga over Charlie. Leon worried the guy might trip on his own tongue, the way it was hanging out.

Jon nudged him with an elbow. "Remember, we saw them come in yesterday."

The day had been so frenetic that Leon hadn't even noticed.

"Her name's Charlene Langston, but according to Debbie at the front desk, she goes by 'Charlie.'"

Charlie *was* a knockout, the honey-blond, voluptuous, full-lipped kind of woman that men's eyes automatically tracked when she walked past. But Leon's gaze kept straying to her mother. Gail Langston was pretty in a sophisticated way, with sleek ash-blond hair and a trim body. The necklace around her throat was an old-fashioned locket with a design he'd never seen before, a mix of copper and silver. But it was her demeanor that drew him to her. Nurses and Elisa's business partner and another woman had entered and exited the room. Charlie and Elisa bantered back and forth like the siblings they were. Gail Langston was quiet. She seemed composed, an oasis of tranquility in the beehive of frantic hospital activity.

"Elisa's going to be okay," he assured her. Holding out his hand, he introduced himself. "Leon Maxwell."

Gail placed her hand in his, and then in Jon's. "I'm delighted to meet the heroes who rescued my daughter."

When his fingers touched hers and he looked into those clear blue eyes, he felt magic. And had he imagined that spark in her gaze?

According to her medical records, Elisa was thirty-two; Charlie looked to be around the same age. Leon was fifty-two, old enough to be their father. And Jon's, too, for that matter, although most of the time his partner seemed more like a younger brother.

Leon's cheeks felt hot. Gail Langston was not at all the type of woman he was usually drawn to. Was this unexpected flutter of excitement what everyone called an "age-appropriate attraction"? He quickly turned his attention from Gail to the hospital bed and his patient. Charlie was razzing her sister about some of the crazy things Elisa had said.

"She says she's been screwed." Charlie reported this with what looked like a teasing smile, but Leon glanced at his partner.

Jon's face registered his uncertainty, too.

"I meant my leg! They put screws in my leg!" Elisa gestured angrily toward the offending leg, which was attached to a traction pulley. "How am I supposed to drive the backhoe with that?"

Charlie looked back at her sister. "And then there was the angel."

Elisa's scratched cheeks darkened with embarrassment. "He *was* real. He left his jacket." She pointed to a windbreaker on a nearby chair.

"She's telling the truth," Jon said. "Some guy called 911. That's how we found her."

"You thought he was an angel," Charlie insisted, grinning at Elisa. "You said he looked like Dad."

Elisa groaned and stared at the ceiling.

Leon assured Elisa that her disorientation was normal after a head injury and hypothermia. After wishing her a speedy recovery, he had to drag Jon away from the hospital to return to the fire station.

"I didn't get Charlie's number," Jon moaned from the passenger seat of the aid truck. "Would I seem like a stalker if I showed up at her house?"

Wondering the same thing about Gail Langston, Leon gripped the steering wheel tightly as he negotiated the corner. "You know that's against the department regs."

Jon groaned. "I can just hear my mom if I hooked up with a blond babe like that."

He followed that statement with a long string of falsetto Korean, imitating his mother. Leon didn't understand a single word, but Jon's tone sounded like a bitter complaint.

Leon tried to focus on his own problem. They were in and out of the hospital practically every day they were on duty. Elisa Langston would be there for at least a day or two more. Did he dare ask the nurses on that floor to let him know when Gail showed up for a visit? Then if they weren't on a call, he and Jon could rush over from the station. He'd have to give the nurses his personal cell phone number.

And what would he and Jon give the lieutenant as an excuse? Gassing up the rig? Maybe checking out that mysterious clunk in the transmission? Like that would fly on the spur of the moment. No, odds were that when the nurse's call came in, they'd be busy treating another break-it-yourselfer who'd superglued his own fingers together. He felt like groaning in frustration, like his partner.

Jon snapped his fingers, jarring Leon out of his reverie. "Maybe I can arrange for our paths to conveniently cross while Charlie's out running errands or something."

Leon turned his head slightly to glance at his partner. "How would you do that?"

Jon shot him a sideways glance. "By following her, of course."

"And that's not stalking?"

They both laughed at the thought of shadowing the Langston women.

Then Leon had a flash of inspiration. "If I remember right, according to the computer info, Langston Green is only one of the family's business locations. There are two flower shop outlets. One in Woodinville, and one in Seattle. The numbers and addresses were on the data sheet for the nursery. Maybe Gail works in one of them."

"You mean Charlie." When Leon didn't reply, Jon turned in his seat to scrutinize his partner. "Ah. You *do* mean Gail. Dude, the woman was wearing a wedding ring."

"Dude," Leon echoed his partner, "that ring was on her right hand." He didn't know whether that was significant, but it seemed hopeful to him. "Her husband died a while ago, remember? The owner of Langston Green?"

Jon's expression remained blank.

Leon sighed. "I keep forgetting you're new to Woodinville. Langston Green used to be a very big deal in this town. Half the population went to Terry Langston's funeral."

"If you say so." Jon pulled his cell phone out of his pocket and started poking it with a finger. "Guess what those Langston flower shops are called? Gail's Flowers in Seattle, and Charlene's Flowers in Woodinville."

"Bingo! We could call the flower shops to express our best wishes for Elisa's recovery."

Jon's brow creased. "That could be a first step. But if Charlie's in the Woodinville shop, then I definitely need to go in and order flowers for my mother." He did the falsetto Korean voice again, this time sounding happy.

"And if Gail's in the Seattle store, I need to drive there to order some for *my* mother." Leon followed this up with his own imitation of a female voice saying, "Well, what a surprise, dear! What could possibly be the occasion? It's not my birthday, it's not Mother's Day . . ."

Jon chuckled. "We'll invent a holiday." He held out a fist.

Leon bumped it with his own.

Jon folded his arms across his chest. "But, Lion Man, how are you going to juggle two women? Won't Karma be jealous?"

Leon clutched the steering wheel so hard his knuckles turned white. "I'm not with Karma. We've never been a couple. Don't ever joke about Karma. Don't mention her name ever again."

Chapter 3

Gail Langston couldn't get her mind off Leon Maxwell. It was crazy, but she'd felt instantly drawn to him, like water wicked up through a straw. Of course she was attracted, she excused herself; she wasn't dead. Leon was a good-looking man somewhere near her age, with thick, closely cropped and carefully parted silver-blond hair. Plus, he'd been neatly dressed in a sharp fire department EMT uniform. Stereotypical hero material.

When he took her hand in the hospital room, she'd realized that he was the first man in a long time who didn't know her as The Widow.

He had been polite and attentive toward Elisa, which was only right—she was his patient. But Gail couldn't help admiring the lines of Leon's back and buns, the tight muscles of his lean frame as he bent over to chat with her injured daughter. Unlike most middle-aged men, Leon Maxwell was trim. And toned. She wouldn't mind spending more time with *that* body.

Then she had blushed, embarrassed that the thought had crossed her brain, and oh so grateful that neither EMT had been watching her face when it did. She fingered the locket at her throat to prevent herself from fanning her hot cheeks, and she was relieved when the two firemen left a few minutes later.

"Why didn't I give that Jon guy my number?" Charlie complained.

"He didn't ask for it," Gail said. "Maybe he's married."

"He wasn't wearing a ring." Charlie twitched her honey-colored mane back over her shoulder. "Dammit, the only man who hasn't slipped me his card lately . . . I'm an idiot."

Gail cleared her throat. "I have an idea. We both have the day off tomorrow. Why don't we drop by the fire station to say thank you? We can take some cookies for the whole crew. It would be the polite thing to do."

Charlie stared at her, surprised. "Mom, that's brilliant! Jon won't think I'm stalking him if you're along. Thanks for looking out for me."

"You're welcome." Gail smiled. Charlie could be a little dense at times.

The next day, they arrived a little after two p.m., just as the aid truck was backing into the station, returning from a call. With a plate of cookies in hand, Gail and Charlie waited by the front desk after asking for the two EMTs.

"They'll be in to write up their report in just a minute," said the pudgy firefighter who welcomed them. He had a comb-over, dispelling the notion that all men in fire department uniforms were drop-dead gorgeous.

Through an open door, they heard catcalls from other voices in the central lounge area as Jon and Leon entered from the garage. "Woo-hoo, aren't you guys *special!* Why do EMTs get all the glory?"

"What the hell?" Jon Park's voice.

"First, You-Know-Who brought pizza for everyone." That line was delivered by a female voice, and Gail was pleased that the station crew included a woman. "She was looking for you, Maxwell."

Gail focused her gaze on the plate of cookies in her hands. Leon Maxwell was a Romeo? She pressed her lips together, tamping down a twinge of disappointment. *Well, okay.* She wasn't really expecting to have a relationship with the guy. For

Charlie's sake, Gail was glad that the reputation belonged to Maxwell, not to Jonathan Park.

Then she heard Leon's response, surprisingly gruff. "Don't let her in here again."

The first male voice said, "You don't want Karma? I'll take her. She's a hottie. And she always brings food. But speaking of hotties, you two have visitors waiting in the foyer."

"Visitors bearing gingersnaps," the bald guy yelled. "Come on out, everyone. And try to be polite for a change."

Four men and two women in fire department uniforms streamed through the doorway into the front office area. On spotting Charlie, Jon positively lit up. Leon dipped his chin and smiled in recognition as he introduced them as the pretty mother and sister of their ambulance patient from two days earlier.

Was there any significance to the fact that Leon had put "pretty" in front of the word "mother" instead of "sister"? Probably not. But it sounded good, anyway.

"Langston?" The balding man, whom Jon had introduced as Conrad, asked. "Like Langston Green?"

"That's our family business," Charlie said. "My sister, Elisa, runs it now."

"Oh yeah," Conrad said. "I remember . . ." His voice drifted away for a moment, no doubt remembering that Terry Langston was dead. He recovered with, "My family always loved that big party in the fall."

"Harvest Fest," Gail supplied. "We hope to revive it again soon."

The conversation thudded to a sad, polite stop there as everyone debated what was appropriate to say next. As the awkward silence dragged out, Gail briefly contemplated running out the door.

After taking a deep breath, Charlie held out the plate of cookies. "Ginger snaps, anyone?"

While the rest of the crew devoured most of the cookies, Jon and Leon gave Gail and Charlie a tour of the station. It didn't take long. Aside from the large garage and equipment bays, the building contained one dining-meeting-classroom area with a huge table surrounded by chairs, a compact kitchen, an exercise room, and a lounge area complete with big-screen TV, Spartan individual sleeping quarters, and group bathrooms.

After the fifteen-minute tour, there seemed nothing left for the four of them to say to one another, or at least nothing that could be said with all the other firefighters listening in. Charlie's gaze had never left Jon Park. She'd eagerly taken his hand when he suggested the tour, and as the two EMTs walked them to the parking lot, Gail noticed her daughter's fingers were still entwined around Jon's.

She squinted her eyes at the sight. Park had better be a decent man. He'd better not be married. Men were always lusting after Charlie, but few were interested in her daughter's brain, or in her tender heart.

At the Lexus, Gail turned to Leon. "Elisa is scheduled to get out of the hospital on Thursday. Can you and Jon come to dinner that evening?"

The two EMTs exchanged glances.

"We're off that day," Leon remarked.

He had beautiful eyes, Gail noticed, fringed with thick black lashes. His irises were mostly gray but held a tint of blue. Soulful eyes.

Gail gave herself a mental slap. Romeo, she reminded herself.

Jon smiled at Charlie. "I'd love to."

"*We'd* love to," Leon corrected.

"Great!" Gail chirped. "We'll make it a 'Welcome Home' party for Elisa, then. Before the quake, she was living at the nursery on her own, but now, with her injuries, she'll need our help."

With the assistance of a pitcher of sangria and flirtatious banter between Charlie and Jon, Elisa's "Welcome Home" dinner passed beyond politeness and into a compatible warmth that Gail had missed over the past two years. Elisa could barely navigate with her new crutches, and yet she foolishly combined the red wine punch with her pain meds. She fell asleep at the table, and Gail and Leon ended up carrying her to bed like she was a toddler.

"This is embarrassing," Gail lamented as she slipped Elisa's arm from her shoulder, letting her stepdaughter slump onto the bed.

"No," Leon said. "Embarrassing is when a guy decides to see whether his you-know-what can fit into a knothole in a piece of firewood, and then he gets stuck and has to call us for help."

"Really?" Gail stared at him, uncertain about how to process that information.

Leon grinned, his cheeks reddening. "Did that actually come out of my mouth? Sorry, TMI. Too much information. And probably too much sangria."

Averting her eyes, she ducked her chin in hopes that he wouldn't notice the smile playing across her lips. She took a minute to pull the bedspread over Elisa and tuck it around her daughter. As they turned toward the door, Gail chanced a sideways glance at Leon.

He had a glint in his eye. "We got that call just yesterday. Sometimes it's hard for an EMT to keep a straight face."

"I guess." She stopped just outside Elisa's doorway. "How did you get him . . . it . . . I mean . . ." She intended to finish the question but couldn't keep from bursting into laughter at the absurdity of the conversation.

Leaning against the walls of the hallway, they laughed together until their eyes watered.

"*What* is going on out there?" Charlie called from the kitchen.

"Nothing," Gail barely managed to gasp, trying to stifle her laughter with a hand pressed to her lips.

When they'd caught their breath again, Leon gently brushed a tear from Gail's cheek. "Can't say anything more. Privacy rules, you know."

"I get it." She started back toward the kitchen.

He shrugged. "You might know the guy."

What an alarming thought. "Good heavens, I hope not!"

That sent them into another gale of laughter. It felt so good. She hadn't really laughed since Terry . . . *Drat.* Why couldn't her brain just let her enjoy the moment?

"Mom?" Charlie's voice queried from down the hall.

"Coming," she called back. But in the minute it took to reach the kitchen table, Charlie had clearly forgotten her concern. Her blond daughter was leaning into Jon, sharing some intimate joke with the younger EMT.

"Why don't you two leave the cleanup to Gail and me?" Leon suggested.

"Oh, that's a rare offer." His dark eyes flashing a note of gratitude, Jon eagerly pulled Charlie to her feet and led her to the living room. "We'd better take it before my partner changes his mind."

Leon was too easy to be with. Gail was overly conscious of the warmth of his fingers when they touched as he helped her clear the table and load the dishwasher. Whenever their eyes met, he gave her a tentative smile, as if he had a secret that he wanted to share with her.

If only he would wrap his muscular body around hers and pin her against the kitchen wall with a burning kiss.

She felt a blush creeping up her face and quickly turned toward the countertop. "Gracious Gail"; that was how people described her. All calm good taste and manners. If they could read her thoughts now, they'd be shocked. *Gracious, Gail! Have you forgotten Terry?*

Jerking open the cupboard door, she pulled the wastebasket from under the sink. "Excuse me a minute."

Scurrying out the back door, she shut it behind her, set down the wastebasket, and then leaned against the side of the house. The moon was nearly full, lending the backyard a silvery glow. The air was surprisingly warm and soft for September. She sucked in several deep, shuddering breaths, fingering the locket at her neck, sliding it back and forth on its silver chain as she tried to regain control of her emotions.

Her long-time friends still treated her like she was so fragile she might break. And then there were the ones who claimed to miss her but always found ways to point out that she no longer fit in. Less than a week ago, as she'd been leaving the grocery store, she'd run into her so-called friend Linda Beyers, whom she hadn't seen since Terry's funeral. Linda had smiled and given her a one-armed hug, saying, "How are you? It's been too long!"

Linda's gaze slid to Gail's hands around the grocery bag she carried. "Oh, Gail, you're still wearing your wedding ring?"

"Yes." The time never seemed right to take it off. "I did move it to my right hand."

"Isn't it about time you started dating?" Linda nodded her head as if to answer the question.

Gail hadn't been on a date for decades. The whole idea seemed preposterous. She shook her head. "I don't think so."

"Did you ever go to that grief support group I recommended?"

"Once." Although it was probably healthy to be reminded that she wasn't the only person who'd lost a spouse, she didn't see what good it would do to spend her time with more sad people.

Linda pushed her hair back from her cheeks, smoothed it

into place. "No hot widowers there you could bond with?"

Gail stared at the other woman. Was *that* supposed to be the purpose of going to a grief group? "Uh, not that I noticed."

Nearly everyone in the group had lost their spouse to a disease, so they'd had more time to prepare, if one could *ever* prepare for that. Only one man had lost his wife suddenly in a car accident. Which he had caused. He was eighty-seven, and between sobs had repeatedly confessed that he should never have been driving. No, Martin had not been date material. Beside all that, Gail was certain she had been the only person in the room who had lost *two* spouses *and* a fiancé. She'd been afraid to share that information. The others might have thought she was some sort of black widow.

"As for dating," she told Linda, "I wouldn't even know where to start."

Linda waved a dismissive hand in the air. "I know exactly what you're going through. After Randy and I divorced, it took me *months* to feel confident enough to get back out there."

A bubble of anger floated up from Gail's gut and filled her mouth with the taste of bile. Linda was equating her divorce after two and a half years of marriage with the *death* of Gail's husband after twenty-three? She pressed her lips together to keep bitter words from spilling out.

"Why don't you try one of the online sites?" Linda blithely suggested. "I could help you with your profile. It would be so nice if you found another man. Then Dave and I could invite you over to dinner parties again. We miss you."

Apparently, Linda's social Ark only took humans in twos; there was no room for a single woman. Saying she was late for an appointment, Gail had excused herself quickly, but now she was still cursing herself for not responding to Linda's verbal slap in the face. Was she truly that worthless on her own?

Had she and Terry excluded unmarried friends from their circle? She didn't really want to examine that history, but now that she thought about it, she no longer had any single friends. She'd lost touch with her college buddies years ago. Likewise with her teaching colleagues. They were probably all married by now, anyway. So no, no single friends. Her daughters Charlie and Elisa didn't count.

Then she searched her brain for married friends and drew an even more alarming blank. Did she have any real friends at all?

All the smiling faces she'd spent time with during the last two decades, all the people she'd met at parties and picnics. They were all *Terry's* friends, she now realized with a start. All those couples had been part of the package deal of marrying Terrence Langston. Husband, home, second daughter, business, friends. She'd been thrilled to find such a complete existence. And now the husband and the so-called friends . . . gone. Even the Langston family businesses were on the ropes.

Third time's the charm. What horse hockey. What was supposed to come *after* the third time? Nothing? The phrase, "Three strikes, you're out," crawled uninvited into her head. Why did everything come in threes, anyway? What a stupid superstition.

The sound of the door opening behind her called her back to the present.

Leon's gray eyes were full of concern. "Is something wrong, Gail?"

He was a single man. He could be a friend. Or maybe even something more. She could love those eyes, that chiseled face, that softly tousled silvery hair, those gentle hands. And she would love a new life.

All crazy thoughts. They'd only just met. Of course, he was charming; he was a player. He probably wasn't attracted to her at all. He was only being kind. When he found out what a train wreck she was, what a mess the whole family was right now, she'd never see Leon Maxwell again.

And even if he was attracted to her—even if they fell in love and created a life together—in a month, a year, twenty years, the cycle could happen all over again. He'd die. And then she'd be alone again with only her guilt for company.

Leon gently touched her forearm. She abruptly realized she was reclining against the house, stuck there against the siding like some sort of zombie. A couple of quick blinks brought her surroundings back into focus. "Everything's fine, Leon." She flashed him a small smile and picked up the wastebasket.

He unfastened the bungee cord across the top of the trash can. "What's the cord for?" he asked as he lifted the lid.

"Raccoon proofing," she said. "Those masked bandits are experts at prying off lids. It's probably only a matter of time before they master bungee cords."

Leon nodded. "I've seen 'em do macramé. And don't ever loan one your cell phone, no matter how innocent that little striped face looks."

She chuckled at the crazy images he'd conjured up. After she dumped in the meager contents of the wastebasket, she tucked it back under her arm. "Thanks for your help, Leon."

Chapter 4

Gail Langston had been widowed only two years ago. That explained why she acted like a wary doe stepping into a clearing, ready to race back into the woods at the first flash of movement.

He'd need to approach carefully. Although he might have already mucked it up at the family dinner at her house. Sharing his tale of the schlong in the knothole was probably not the smartest move he'd ever made, although Gail seemed to enjoy the story. But then, what was that awkward dash into the backyard with the almost-empty wastebasket?

The Langston home was modest, he'd been surprised to see. After all, they owned the huge nursery and two flower shops. But apparently all three women worked, and the fact that they worked with their hands made Gail seem more approachable than if she'd been a society lady spending her days doing yoga and organizing fundraising events for charity.

He was pleased when Gail agreed to join him on a double date with Jon and Charlie. He and Jon had chosen an action adventure movie, during which it became clear that the attraction between Charlie and his partner was nearing the flashpoint. Leon had been surprised that all heads in the movie theater didn't turn their way, tracking the cloud of pheromones fogging the air. After the foursome returned to the Langston house, the younger couple zoomed off in Jon's car, leaving Leon to walk Gail to her door.

He stepped so close that his breath lifted her fine ash-blond hair. She smelled like a mix of lilac and lemon—was that possible? "Your locket is beautiful," he said, peering down at the necklace at her throat. "It looks like an antique."

Lowering her gaze, she raised her right hand and pressed the locket to her chest. "It is."

"I've noticed you wear it often."

After an awkward few seconds, she raised her eyes and told him, "It was a gift from my husband for our twentieth wedding anniversary."

"No wonder it's special, then." Competing with her dead husband was going to be an even higher hurdle than he'd feared. "Dinner tomorrow?" he suggested.

Her blue eyes went wide. "Just the two of us?"

He made a show of glancing up and down the quiet residential street before he turned back to meet her gaze. "Think we could risk an evening without the chaperones?"

Gail hesitated a second before answering.

Say yes. He wanted more time to get to know her. Ten minutes with Karma felt like pressing his hand onto a hot stove burner; he was embarrassed that he'd fallen for that witch, even if it was only once. Clearly, his mind had not been engaged at the time. Spending time with Gail Langston promised to be like slipping into cool water, tranquil and soothing. He gave her a smile that he hoped was encouraging.

Gail dipped her chin. "Let's do it."

His brain knew she meant dinner, but his lower body reacted to a wishful interpretation. He had to lean over to chastely kiss her good night instead of hugging her close.

Chapter 5

The next day, Gail stood in front of her closet, dithering about what to wear on their first solo date. All Leon had mentioned was dinner. The blue cocktail dress? The black-and-white print? Blouse and skirt? Slacks? Heels? She slid the hangers back and forth until the whole question of what to wear seemed completely ridiculous. In fact, after twenty-three years of marriage, the idea of dating seemed ridiculous. Should she call off the dinner?

And do what? Sit home alone, again? Infinitely worse. Or at least she hoped she'd still think so after tonight.

Finally, she settled on the aqua-colored dress. Terry had loved that dress. She hadn't worn it since their last date over two years ago. With a jewel neckline and long sleeves, it was demure enough, but the slinky knit fabric clung to her curves. She looked good in it; she felt good in it.

She zipped it and regarded herself in the mirror. Terry's favorite dress.

No. She couldn't do this.

The doorbell rang.

She had to do this. The doorbell chimed again.

"Sorry, Terry," she murmured to her reflection.

Three loud raps sounded on the front door.

"Just a second!" she yelled. She added beige pumps and dangling gold earrings. *There. Done.*

"Wowza," Leon said when she answered the door. His gaze traveled appreciatively from her face to her ankles. He wore gray jeans, an ivory fisherman's sweater, and a black leather jacket.

Anxiety churned through her stomach. "Am I overdressed?"

"Not as far as I'm concerned. You look like ..." He hesitated. "Well, I was going to say a million bucks, but how trite can you get? You look like Ariel."

What? "The mermaid?"

"Yeah."

"Ariel has red hair."

"Does she? I was referring to that killer sea-green dress." He held out his hand, guided her down the front steps, and pulled her toward his RAV4. "Your pumpkin awaits, princess."

She laughed. "You must have a daughter."

"Nope, just star-struck nieces."

"You're mixing up all the Disney stories."

He pulled open the passenger door. "Variety is the salsa of life, don't you think?"

She slid into the seat. "Where are we going?"

"One of my favorite restaurants." He rounded the SUV and slid into the seat beside her. "Next time, you get to choose."

Gail turned her gaze to the side window. He'd already decided there would be a next time? Should she consider that presumptuous, or hopeful? They passed Rosetti's, the poshest place in Woodinville. As they neared Evergreen, the other fancy restaurant, Gail caught a glimpse of a couple through the front window of the eatery. Seated across from a blond woman was an auburn-haired man, and for a second, it felt as if she were watching herself and Terry having dinner. She bit her lip as they passed and then pulled her vision back to the road ahead.

Where were they going? Just when she decided Leon was headed for Kirkland, the adjacent city, he suddenly swung right into a gravel parking lot in front of a nondescript brick building. The painted sign over the door labeled it, THE BAYOU.

It was a brewpub. Gail's heels clicked an embarrassingly noisy rhythm along the raised cedar walkway from the parking lot, then tapped more softly across the scuffed floor. Behind glass panels, huge stainless-steel vats guarded one side of the main room, while the opposite side was occupied by a long antique bar. The furniture scattered across the wide-planked floor was heavily lacquered pine, square tables paired with chairs, longer tables flanked by picnic benches. Menus stood upright between salt and pepper shakers and napkin holders.

On the walls hung huge photographs of snowy mountain peaks, mossy cypresses overhanging murky swamps, and glistening ocean waves, interspersed with colorful pieces of gear—parachutes, hang-gliding sails, and kayak paddles. In the far corner was a well-scuffed dance floor and a setup for a band. The sign on the drum read, RAGGED RIDGE RUNNERS.

Most of the patrons wore jeans or khakis with tees or sweaters. Several pairs of eyes swiveled in Gail's direction as they passed through the tap room. Hers was the only skirt in the place aside from the scrap of material the server wore under her apron.

"Don't mind them," Leon murmured in her ear. Grinning, he called out to a man standing at the bar, "Hey, Jonesy, stop lusting after my date."

The man raised his beer glass. "Aw, yours is so much better looking than *mine*." He rolled his eyes theatrically at the bearded friend at his side, who snorted and swiftly whacked Jonesy on the arm, sloshing his beer onto the floor.

"Bet your date is less violent, too," Jonesy commented, rubbing his arm.

"I'm counting on it," Leon retorted. Placing his hand at the small of Gail's back, he guided her to an empty table in the corner.

Gail slid into her chair. How awkward. She rubbed her fingers nervously against an itchy spot at her waist. Why hadn't she asked Leon for a hint about what to wear? She'd dressed for the sort of place Terry always took her—a ritzy restaurant with expensive wine and seafood.

The young server flitted over and landed beside them, snatching an order pad from the pocket of her apron. "What'll it be?"

Gail hadn't yet had a chance to pick up the menu, let alone read it. "You obviously come here often," she said to Leon. "I eat pretty much everything. You pick for me."

"Sure thing." He turned to the server. "Two ESBs and two black-and-blues with spinach salads. House dressing." He smiled at Gail. "Okay?"

"Sounds great." Aside from the spinach salads, she had no idea what he had just ordered. The words sounded more like an industrial accident than a meal.

The ESBs turned out to be beers, dark and frothy and served in heavy glass mugs. On the rare occasions that she drank a beer, it was a light beer, one of the interchangeable brands that were everywhere. She lifted the frosty mug in front of her and took a tentative sip. The taste was smoky and bitter and mellow all at the same time.

"Like it?" Leon asked.

"I do."

"You sound surprised."

"I am." She took another sip before setting the mug down. "It's delicious."

The black-and-blues turned out to be huge grilled buffalo burgers with blue cheese oozing from beneath the buns, and fresh spinach and tomato salads on the side. She stared at her plate, debating whether to pick up the giant burger or cut it with her knife and fork. Now another spot was itching, this one over her right shoulder at the back of her neck. She rubbed her fingers over it. What was wrong with her?

Leon's brow furrowed. "If you don't like the food, you can

get something else."

"No. It looks wonderful. I'm just . . . you know . . . first date." Yeesh, she sounded like a twelve-year-old. "I mean, first date alone."

Oh, crap, that sounded even worse, like she was afraid to be alone with him. Now she sounded uptight and prissy. She scratched the irritation at her waistline. Was she about to break into hives or something? *Get a grip,* she told herself.

Leon's confusion registered on his face. Her embarrassment deepened. He probably took women out on first dates every week; he was the fire station Romeo. Hastily she added, "What I really mean is, I'm afraid that I'm going to drip grease and cheese all over myself."

He smoothed his index finger over the back of her hand. "If that happens, I'll take you back to the fire station afterward, and we can hose each other down."

She laughed. After taking the precaution of tucking her napkin into her neckline, she picked up the burger. She hadn't eaten red meat for years, let alone a burger with the works. It tasted as good as the beer. They chatted about how long they'd lived in Woodinville (thirty years for him, twenty-five for her), about how long he'd worked for the fire department (thirty years, again), and about the area's slow recovery from the earthquake. She was surprised to discover he was originally from Kansas. She'd never met anyone from Kansas before.

Then he made the mistake of asking, "How is Elisa doing?"

Her throat closed up. She smoothed her skirt over her thighs as she reflected on what to say.

She was frightened for her adopted daughter. Elisa had lost so much in her life. And now, an employee Elisa cared deeply about, a teenager named Timo Martinez, had been missing since the earthquake.

An insurance investigator was also sniffing around, hinting that Elisa was intentionally running the nursery into the ground. And then, less than a week ago, the coup de grâce: the main building that had housed Elisa's apartment and the Langston Green office had burned to the ground. That building had been the original homestead, owned by the Langston family for generations. The fire investigator had deemed it arson, and Elisa was the main suspect.

Even with her broken leg in a heavy cast, the poor girl was working day and night to revive the Langston Green nursery. She'd stubbornly insisted on renting an RV and moving back to the site. But the business seemed to be in a death spiral.

She could tell by the searching look in Leon Maxwell's eyes that he knew all that. Of course he did; his station had been called to the fire. The itch at the back of her neck was getting worse. Gail flexed her shoulders backward and forward, trying to make the irritation go away.

"Forgive me." Leon stroked his fingers across the back of her hand. "I didn't mean to put a damper on our party."

"It's okay." She told him, "Elisa's getting around surprisingly well on her crutches." Not the answer he was looking for, she was sure.

Thankfully, he played along. "I could tell that she's a fighter."

Then they abruptly fell into a conversational crevasse. Gail awkwardly busied herself with small bites of her burger and salad and slow sips of her beer. Leon's plate was already empty, and his glass held less than half an inch of amber liquid.

When his cell phone conveniently buzzed, she was grateful.

"Excuse me." He pulled the phone from his rear pants pocket. The caller ID was large enough that she could make out the word "Karma." The name she'd heard in the fire station. Leon grimaced, pressed a button to silence the buzzing, and shoved the phone back into his pocket. "Sorry."

"No worries," she said. "Who is Karma?"

A flash of emotion passed over his face. Annoyance? Alarm? She didn't have time to decipher the expression before it was gone.

"I'm sorry," she murmured, shifting her glance toward the bar. "It's none of my business."

He gently touched her shoulder. "It's okay, Gail. She's nobody you need to worry about."

Strange answer. Focusing on her plate, she speared a cherry tomato with her fork. Obviously, Karma was a woman he was involved with. She debated with herself for a few seconds over how she felt about Leon dating several women at once. They were both adults; they weren't really in a relationship. This was probably a good thing. It took the pressure off, knowing he wasn't focused only on her.

"Are you okay, Gail?"

She looked up into his gray-blue eyes and smiled. "Yes. I'm having a great time. This food is delicious." Picking up the last of her burger, she shoved it into her mouth.

He scratched a fingertip across his lower jaw as he regarded her. "I just realized I've been doing most of the talking. I want to hear Gail Langston's history."

Gail Langston's history? *Three dead men?* She shook her head. "Too boring. I want to know more about *you*."

After squinting his eyes in curiosity for a second, he relaxed and said, "I'm an open book. Ask me anything."

In her teens and twenties, dating seemed natural, spontaneous. At this age, the dance of getting to know each other seemed so calculated. She sensed she wasn't playing the game very well, tears threatening one moment and asking questions that were too personal the next. Still, every relationship had to start somewhere, didn't it?

"How old are you?" she asked.

"Fifty-two."

She groaned. "Good heavens. I'm a cougar."

He quirked an eyebrow. "How old are *you*?"

She blushed. Well, she'd already admitted she was older. "Fifty-three."

He sat back in his chair, smiling. "Well then, enjoy your predator status now because you'll only be a cougar to me for a few more months."

"*Rowr,*" she responded.

"Next question, kitty."

Maybe Karma was an ex-wife. Gail put an elbow on the table, edged closer, and asked in a quiet tone, "Have you ever been married?"

He leaned so close to her ear she could feel his warm breath on her cheek as he murmured, "Never even came close."

He sat back, his eyes fixed on her.

Never? The man was over fifty and he'd never been married or even engaged? She hoped her expression didn't show how appalled she was. What was wrong with him?

He laid his hand on top of hers on the table. "I'm not a serial killer. Or a child molester. I don't wear women's underwear. And I haven't lived with my parents since I was eighteen."

Her cheeks flamed. She pulled her hand out from under his and rested it on the handle of her beer mug. "None of those things crossed my mind."

His eyes crinkled at the corners as he grinned. "Then you're the first woman I've met who didn't wonder whether I was some sort of freak. The simple truth is that I've never found the woman I wanted to spend the rest of my life with."

He couldn't have picked more unfortunate words. Keith, Mark, and Terry *had* spent the rest of their lives with her. The *last* of their lives.

For pity sake, now she was losing it again. The itch at her waistline was growing more irritating by the second.

"Excuse me." She rose to her feet and grabbed her purse.

"I'll be back."

In the restroom stall, she unzipped her dress and peeled it halfway down, twisting it around, looking for the offending labels or tags that were driving her crazy. There, at the back, stapled into the shoulder seam. Not a sewn-in label at all. A small piece of paper.

Yahoo, my favorite dress! it said. She checked the left side along her waistline. Another note. *What are we celebrating?*

Her breath caught in her chest. Terry's handwriting. *Oh God, not now.* She pried out the staples with a fingernail and pushed the notes into her purse, then closed her eyes and took ten deep, slow breaths. Another woman entered the stall next to hers. Gail zipped up her dress and moved to the sink, where she splashed her face with cold water and freshened her makeup. Leaning toward the mirror, she told her reflection, "You can do this."

"Damn straight, girl." The other woman was standing behind her now. She appeared to be about the age of Gail's mother. "Whatever it is, you can handle it."

Gail smiled uncertainly at this encouragement from a perfect stranger. "Thanks."

As she slipped her lipstick back into her purse, Gail again caught a glimpse of Terry's notes and hurriedly zipped the clutch shut.

When she slid into her seat, Leon asked, "Are you alright?" His gaze was focused too intently on her face.

"Yes, of course." To avoid looking at him, she gulped down the last of her beer. As she clunked her empty mug on the table, the band struck up a loud western tune and all eyes turned in the direction of the music.

Couples spilled out onto the dance floor. Leon stood up and grabbed her hand.

She pulled back. "I can't."

"Yes, you can." He tugged her to her feet.

She wobbled a bit as she rose from her chair for the second time. No wonder she usually drank light beer; the effect of that ESB was kicking in. "Easy for you to say; you're not wearing three-inch heels."

"Then lose 'em." His eyes dared her.

She glanced at the dance floor. Couples in denim and tees, cowboy boots and sandals were bouncing around the smooth wooden planks.

What the heck. She peeled off her pumps and nudged them under the table. As they maneuvered toward the dance floor, Leon brushed shoulders with the waitress and ordered another round of beer.

The band moved into a fast song with a driving beat. The chorus seemed to be, "If Bubba Can Dance, Well, I Can Too!" and every time it came around, everyone on the dance floor shouted the refrain and made appropriately crazy movements to show off their own abilities.

Gail couldn't have asked for a better icebreaker. At first, she felt gawky and graceless, which at least matched the frantic movements around her. But then she found her rhythm, shaking her hips and swinging her arms. Leon side-stepped and boogied around her, a grin a mile wide on his face.

The band segued into another song about dancing and drinking José Cuervo. Leon caught her hand and pulled her in close, and they swayed and stepped together in rapid harmony. He spun her out in a twirl, and when he reeled her back in against his chest, she laughed out loud along with him. She'd forgotten how much she loved to dance.

What are we celebrating?

Life, Terry. Life.

And then, without warning, Leon transformed into Keith, and she was her eighteen-year-old self, showing off her new black lace bra under her sheer white blouse, shaking her denim miniskirt in the local dive in front of a group of admiring uniforms watching from the bar. Keith, her golden-haired helicopter pilot. Her first ghost. Gail closed her eyes and raised her hands above her head, trying to dispel the intrusive memory.

She and Terry had never danced like this. They'd done slow dances, waltzes, and foxtrots, but they'd never let it all go. They never just relished rocking out. Or maybe nobody called it "rocking out" anymore. And this was country, not rock and roll, anyway.

As the tequila song ended, Leon murmured, "I knew you were a dancing girl."

The music changed to a slower two-step, and Leon put his free hand on her waist again. Keith. Terry. Memories of strong male hands guiding her on the dance floor. She lowered her eyes and focused on her partner's shoulder, but she could feel Leon's gaze on her face as they glided around the floor, their hands in formal position. She couldn't help noticing that the couples around them were pasted together like mating frogs.

As the song progressed, her face grew hot, and she knew that her cheeks would soon be beet red. Halfway through the dance, Leon whispered, "Want to take a break?"

She loved that he was so perceptive; she hated that her emotions were that readable. Back at the table, they sipped the two new beers waiting for them and listened through a slow country tune about a guy missing his girl and dying inside and nobody knowing about it but him.

Dying.

Tears were again threatening to drip down her own cheeks when the band moved on to another fast tune and Leon pulled her back out to the floor.

Two beers had made her tipsy, but the buzz felt good. She was so tired of being sad. She closed her eyes and let the music course through her. Sweat trickled down her backbone and her dangling earrings tickled her neck as she moved her head to the beat.

At ten forty-five, the band packed up to make way for an incoming group. When she and Leon left the brewpub at eleven p.m., she carried her heels instead of wearing them. On their way to the parking lot, Gail spotted a familiar blonde.

"Mom?" Charlie, dressed in skin-tight jeans and a tailored silk blouse, stared at her as if she hadn't seen Gail in a decade instead of just this morning. *"Mom?"*

Gail raised a hand. "Guilty as charged."

Standing beside Charlie, one arm around her waist, was Leon's EMT partner. Jonathan Park held out a hand toward Leon, and the two firemen fist-bumped before Jon pulled Charlie toward the brewpub entrance. Gail couldn't quite read her daughter's face before she turned away. Confusion? Disappointment? Charlie's expression had definitely not been joyful.

Gail was not prepared to walk through the gravel parking lot in her bare feet, so at the end of the concrete walkway, she put a hand on Leon's arm to steady herself and raised a foot to pull on a high heel. Instead, Leon swung her into his arms to carry her the few yards to the SUV. Her bare feet dangled in the cool breeze and her shoes swung from her free hand while her other hand clung to Leon's neck. His leather jacket was unzipped, and she was hyperaware of the intoxicating hardness of his chest muscles against her body. She could feel his heart beating through his sweater. Could he feel hers?

A horn blared, gravel screeched, and they both swiveled to stare in horror at the white Subaru wagon that slammed to a stop only inches away from Leon's thighs. Although it was dark, the sun visor was pulled down and Gail couldn't see the driver. The horn blasted again. Then Leon trotted swiftly across the lane and deposited Gail in the passenger seat of his RAV4.

The driver of the offending car floored the accelerator and

peeled out of the lot, leaving behind a cloud of dust that drifted across the parked cars.

Gail clung to Leon's arm for a second after he had set her down. "That was close." She coughed. "That driver came out of nowhere."

Leon scowled at the lingering dust behind them. "Probably a drunk. You okay?"

She nodded. He crossed the front to slide into his seat and put the RAV4 into reverse, backing out of the tight parking space.

On the drive back to Gail's house, they both listened to the songs on his sound system without talking. The near miss in the parking lot had clearly rattled Leon. He drove cautiously, checking for traffic from side streets at all the stops and glancing frequently at the rearview mirror, although traffic was so light there was little reason to worry about tailgaters.

Gail used the lack of conversation to fret about Charlie. Did her daughter think she didn't deserve to have a good time? Did Charlene Langston think her mother was acting inappropriately for a widow? *Was* she acting inappropriately?

Leon opened the car door for her and walked her to the front porch. After she unlocked the door and slid it open an inch, she turned to say good night. A car passed, gunning its motor. Leon's gaze tracked it down the street before he turned back to her.

"I had a blast," he said.

She smiled weakly. "I did, too."

It was true. Why did she feel so guilty?

He hesitated, staring at the light seeping out the window from the living room. For a minute, she was afraid he would ask to come in. Instead, he cupped her shoulder with one hand while he briefly trailed the fingertips of his other hand against her neck. His warmth enveloped her, and she fought the urge to flatten herself against his strong chest and embrace him with her whole body.

Leon's fingers moved from her neck to her chin. He gently tipped up her face and kissed her softly on the lips.

"Gail," he murmured. "Life is for the living."

Then he pulled away and walked back to his car. As he yanked open the door, he shouted, "I'll be back."

Oh, she hoped so.

But Leon had never been married. She'd been married twice; nearly three times. Keith. Mark. Terry. Three lovers. Three dead men.

Inside the house, Gail locked the deadbolt and leaned back against the door, listening to Terry's old grandfather clock tick off the long slow minutes. The house seemed way too quiet for a place inhabited by so many ghosts.

Chapter 6

Damn Karma. Leon gripped the wheel so tightly his fingers ached, then snorted at the words that passed through his head. Even the woman's name was crazy; he'd bet it was really Karla or Karmen and she'd changed it to Karma to be more dramatic. Had she been driving past The Bayou and spotted his SUV in the parking lot, or had she followed them to the brewpub? Either scenario was freaky.

Thank God the car racing past Gail's house hadn't been Karma's; she hadn't followed them and witnessed that kiss at the front door. Although maybe after seeing him with Gail, Karma would finally get the idea that their relationship was over. Not that it had ever really existed in the first place.

He pulled into the parking lot of his apartment complex, turned off the engine, and sat for a minute, trying to decide how to get Karma off his back.

He checked his watch. Eleven twenty. Karma would still be up. He selected her name from the list on his phone. Instead of a hello, he got voicemail. Even better than talking to her. After her chirpy greeting finished, he said, "Karma, I know that was you in the parking lot. I don't ever want to see you do anything like that again. I don't want to see you again, period. You need to get on with your life and leave me alone to get on with mine." He took a breath, debating what to say next. Finally, he simply said, "Goodbye," and pressed "End."

Taking another breath, he tapped in Gail's number. It rang several times before she picked up, and he began to wonder whether he was being rude. Was she already asleep?

"Hello?" Her voice sounded uncertain. Didn't she have caller ID?

"It's me, Leon. I just wanted to say that I'm thinking of you. I had a great time tonight eating and dancing with you. I loved that kiss. And I want to do all of that a lot more."

There was a brief hesitation before she said, "Thank you, Leon. I'm going to have sweet dreams tonight."

Her words sounded kind of formal but encouraging at the same time. He wished her good night and ended the call. The way she'd danced told him that her careful poise hid a complex woman. He was eager to find out more about her.

He trotted up the stairs to his apartment and opened the door. Shrugging out of his jacket, he walked into his bedroom, flicked on the light.

And nearly jumped out of his skin.

"Hello, lover." Karma struck a pose, leaning back against the pillows on his bed. The sheet slipped down, revealing her full, bare breasts.

His heart took a few seconds to recover its normal beat. "How did you get in here?"

He knew he'd locked the door; he'd used his key just a minute ago to get in.

She pursed her lips and gazed slyly up at him through her lashes. "I told the manager I'd forgotten my key. He knows I'm your girlfriend, remember?" Then she slid both hands behind her head, exhibiting even more of her breasts.

He tossed his jacket onto the dresser. "No, Karma, you're not my girlfriend."

A darkness flashed over her face but was quickly replaced by a careful smile. "Leo, I know you're not the kind of man who takes advantage of a girl and then dumps her."

"You know my name is Leon."

"But I like Leo so much better, don't you? Like Leo

DiCaprio." She patted the sheet beside her. "Come on in. Anyone can tell that Green Dress is frigid; all you have to do is look at her. We both know you and I are *hot* together."

He clenched his jaw. How the hell had he ever gotten into this mess? One beer too many on a lonely evening, a woman in the bar coming on to him. She hadn't been any more drunk than he was that night when he'd brought her home. He hadn't taken advantage of her. He hadn't made her any promises. Why wouldn't she just go away?

"You were certainly eager enough the first time," she purred. "And I've still got a lot of tricks to show you."

"Karma, please get out of my bed. Get dressed. And then get out of my apartment."

She frowned. "You don't want to treat me like that."

He clenched his fists. "You want me to pick you up and throw you out?"

"Naked?" She laughed. "Think of the tales the neighbors would tell. And then I'd have no choice but to tell the police about our little lovers' spat, and with domestic violence laws these days . . ."

She let the suggestion hang in the air between them. There was no way to drag clothes onto her, and she was right, there was no question about who would be arrested if he tossed a naked woman out onto the landing. He could lose everything. Grabbing a throw from the couch, he strode back out into the night.

When he woke up the next morning, his right leg was numb and his neck ached from sleeping in the car. A sheet of paper, stuck beneath a wiper, fluttered from his windshield. On one side was his electric bill. The other side held only an imprint of red lips and a sketch it took his exhausted brain a few minutes to decipher. Karma was no artist, but next to the lipsticked kiss she'd laid on the bill, she'd drawn a hand with the middle finger extended.

Chapter 7

When Leon didn't call her again, Gail wondered what she'd said, or not said, during that brief good-night call after their date at The Bayou. Whatever it was, she'd clearly failed some sort of test. Had she been too cool, too stiff during the evening? Too weepy? Maybe in the beginning, but as the evening had progressed . . . No, she hadn't been cool at all. The memory of how she'd drunk two beers and then danced barefoot, gyrating like a teenager, was mortifying now. Had Leon expected an invitation to her bed after that wanton display? She'd wanted to, and the memory of that was even more embarrassing. Would there have been another date if they'd had sex? Or would she be feeling used and discarded now?

Had she made a fool out of herself with Leon? He could take his pick of women. *See, Linda,* she mentally told her former friend. *Like I said, I'm not ready.*

Forget dating, she told herself, and focused again on her plodding schedule, never knowing when she'd be assaulted by a memory of her former life. A week later, on a sunny Saturday at the end of September, she was in the garden, weeding, when she noticed that the azalea bush in the backyard had bloomed again. Terry had planted that azalea for her on their twenty-first wedding anniversary. Confused by a week of temperate autumn weather, the plant had produced several rosettes of creamy, deep-throated flowers, each one perfect, edged and freckled with a deep rose pink, like an exotic orchid. September was supposed to be a time for harvest, not for

Spring-like blooms.

At the nursery, her daughter Elisa was selling gold and rust chrysanthemums and trees with multicolored fall foliage. Elisa was also determined to revive Harvest Fest at Langston Green to prove to the community that the nursery was making a comeback. Harvest Fest had been Terry's big party in autumn, his favorite time of year.

Which coincided with the time he had died two years ago. When she cradled one of the lovely azalea blossoms in her hand, she felt the cool, all-too-familiar fingers of sorrow clutching at her heart.

When the doorbell rang, she answered with a garden trowel in her hand and tears streaming down her face.

Leon stood on her front porch, freshly shaved and handsome. "I was afraid you'd say no if I called first," he explained.

He wore his leather jacket again, this time over jeans and a black T-shirt. His gaze wandered from her dirt-covered gloves to her wet cheeks. "Watering the flowers?"

She couldn't tell him about the azalea. He'd think her brain had fermented. Wiping away tears with the back of a garden glove, she murmured, "No worries. Sometimes a sad memory just sneaks up on me."

He rested his fingers on her shoulder and studied her face. Embarrassed by the scrutiny, she twisted away and cast her gaze into the blurry distance.

Pulling the trowel from her grasp, he laid it on the table just inside the door. "I know exactly what you need."

That sounded suggestive. She was not in the mood for a come-on from any man. "Leon," she protested feebly. "I'm not fit for human company today."

He made a snorting noise, pinched a clump of dirt out of her hair, grabbed her hand, and began to tow her outside.

She dug in her heels, pulling back. "Wait, my purse—"

"No need."

"My house key?"

Sighing, he reversed direction but didn't let go of her hand. Together, they moved back through the front door. "Lock the door."

As soon as she'd grabbed the key and locked the door, he pulled her to his SUV and pushed her into the passenger seat.

"Are you kidnapping me?"

He waved a hand in the air. "It's a glorious day. Trust me."

Oh, hell, she thought. *Why not?* While Leon focused on the road, driving a little too hurriedly for her taste, Gail worked at dragging her mind from the past and Terry's azalea to the present and her current surroundings. The suburbs quickly gave way to the countryside, and in twenty-five minutes they pulled over next to a van alongside the river. Grabbing her hand again, Leon led her down the bank toward a group of people standing around a huge rubber raft. Two other men and the two women she'd met at the fire station were selecting heavy rubber overalls under the direction of a river guide who looked like he was still in high school.

She stopped Leon with a hand on his forearm. "What is this?"

The tallest man turned toward them and boomed, "Lion Man! You decided to join us after all."

"Yep." Leon tugged her down to the group. "This is Gail. She's going, too."

"Yes!" The two female firefighters pumped their fists in the air. "More estrogen for the team!"

That was flattering, but they all looked so fit, so eager to brave the river. The dark-green water swirled in lazy loops around rocks that lined the far bank. And up ahead she saw more rocks in the middle of the stream. That water was glacial melt from the Cascades, she knew. Ice cold.

"I shouldn't," she mumbled to Leon. "I don't think I can."

One eyebrow rose. "You had something more interesting to do today?"

Sob into the laundry? Clean the house again? Mope for a few more hours? He had a point. Pulling her hand from his, she walked to the pile of rubber overalls next to the river guide. "You think any of these will fit me?"

In quick order she found herself stuffed into heavy coated overalls, oversize boots, a waterproof jacket, and a life vest, then perched on an inflated rubber fender with a paddle in her hands.

As the raft left the shore, every muscle in her body was clenched. The guide had positioned her on the right rubber bumper, behind Leon. The pose felt awkward and unsafe, with her feet inside the boat and her torso twisted sideways to dip the paddle into the water. But the raft glided along easily, slipping beneath the overhanging trees through clear dappled water, with only an occasional rise and fall over unseen rocks beneath the surface.

Leon's smooth paddling seemed to indicate that he was an old hand at river rafting. She was admiring the trim of his shoulders and the muscles shifting under his sleeves when he paused his even strokes and turned to look at her over his shoulder. "I'm glad you're here, Gail."

She smiled back. "Thanks for dragging me out."

Then she lost her rhythm as her paddle blade dragged in the water, upsetting her balance. She might have fallen overboard had Leon not reached back and taken hold of her thigh with a firm hand to steady her. She gasped and shook her head at her klutziness. He laughed and focused again on his own paddling.

Leon was right, it was a glorious day. The guide pointed out bald eagles clutching branches overhead. The birds stared intently at the river, waiting for an unwary fish to rise to the top. Sunlight filtered through boughs of dark evergreens and bright-yellow-leafed alders. On the surrounding hills, the vine maples boasted multiple shades of red, from crimson to mulberry. After a mile of gentle paddling, the knots between her shoulder blades began to loosen. She started to relax and enjoy the banter among the group of friends. She couldn't remember the guide's name, but she recalled that the balding firefighter was Conrad and the bearded one had been introduced as another Jon or John something-or-other. The women firefighters were Stacey and April.

Then she noticed a chattering sound ahead.

"Rapids?" April turned her head toward the guide sitting on the back bumper, one hand clasped firmly around the stick that controlled the trailing wooden rudder.

The guide nodded. "Racerock Falls, only a small drop. Paddle now, everyone!"

They all leaned into their paddles. The front of the raft dipped over the falls and then bumped up, sloshing a wave of water across Leon's thighs and into Gail's face. Leon turned briefly to flash a grin at her. She wasn't sure what expression was on her face. There was no time to talk.

"Eee-haw!" one of the guys shouted as they again dropped down and bounced back up. "Bring on the real action!"

"Coming up," the guide shouted. "The *S* curves, and then the Devil's Eyeball. Right side, paddles up. Left side, paddle hard. Now!"

Gail wanted to grab onto something as the boat spun around, but there was nothing except for the emergency rope threaded through eyes along the top of the bumper, and curling her fingers around that did little for her sense of security.

Then the guide was yelling for the right side to paddle like mad, and she had no time to think about anything else. Ahead she saw waves curling around huge boulders. The smooth rushing stretch in-between those rocks had to be the top of a waterfall.

The current pulled them toward a giant rock on the right. Her heart was in her throat. She could see no safe place ahead; they were going to smash into the monster boulder.

"Harder!" the guide yelled. "Everyone now, paddle as fast as you can."

She focused on driving her paddle into the water as powerfully as she could. If she was going to die, at least she'd go down doing her part.

The raft rode a water wave halfway up the monster rock, spun sideways, spun again to straighten, and then was sucked into the fastest water at the top of the falls. For what seemed like minutes, they hung suspended in midair over a giant whirlpool.

Then they dropped. Gail knew she was shrieking, but her voice was lost among the crowd as all the paddlers screamed. A roaring wave crashed over her head, and she was washed into the center of the raft. She was trapped under the surging water for what seemed like an eternity. Her lungs burned. She could see nothing but a green blur. The rubber beneath her feet bounced like a trampoline, and then the raft surged upward as if it were a river creature with a will of its own.

When she emerged from the icy water back into the sunshine, she expected to be the only one left in the raft. She was astounded to find that everyone was still on board. Six of them flopped like beached salmon on the raft's slippery floor. The guide, amazingly enough, was still perched in the back with his hand clenched around the tiller, water streaming from his hair down his face.

Leon hauled himself back into paddling position, slicked his hands over his face and silver hair to squeegee away the water, then grabbed her hands and pulled her back up onto the raft bumper beside him. His eyes were bright. "What a rush, huh?"

"That's one way of putting it." *Terrifying* was another. Pushing her dripping bangs out of her eyes, she tugged her twisted life vest back into place.

Then the guide shouted, "Paddle both sides! Now!"

Thankfully, the next set of rapids was much less dramatic, but there was no time for further discussion. After a last reasonably tranquil passage through ripples, they beached the raft on a sandy shore where the transport van and other employees from the rafting company waited.

"Nice ride," the bearded John or Jon commented. "But nothing like the Nahatlatch, eh, Leon?"

Gail shot a questioning look at Leon.

"British Columbia," he told her. "We flipped, and the whole raft load went for a swim in the rapids there. This trip may not make as good a story as nearly dying in the Nahatlatch River, but trust me, this was a lot more fun."

He slid easily over the edge of the raft into the knee-deep water and waded to shore to help the guide unload supplies.

"Catch!" Stacey yelled, tossing a small dry bag to Leon.

He grabbed for it, but she'd thrown it too high and it sailed over his shoulder to land behind him on the shore with a crunch.

"Oops." Leon grinned. "Sorry I dropped your lunch, Stace."

"Nah," she said. "That was yours. You're getting as klutzy as Conrad. Remember the catfish?"

"Hey!" Conrad yelped. "That fish bit me."

Obviously, the fire station group had been together on many adventures. Adrenaline junkies. Which, she supposed, was what most firefighters were at heart. Eagerly anticipating the next moment that the siren went off.

She had never craved danger and drama. Sirens to her meant trouble, some poor soul dead or dying. Adrenaline junkies often did not live to a ripe old age. They were always exciting to be with, but did she really want to get involved with one again?

As she exited the raft with her paddle still in hand, she caught her huge borrowed rubber boot on the rope lining the bumper and fell face first into the icy river water. Her outstretched hand sank into soft mud as she tried to brace herself against the bottom, and she had to tug it free before she could get back to the surface. She staggered upright, spitting water, her right hand slimed to the wrist with gray river mud.

She had to swish her arm in the river before she could push her hair out of her eyes. Oh God, her hair! Without her smoothing iron, she'd look like a drowned poodle. An aging drowned poodle. She couldn't believe her bad luck. She hadn't fallen out of the boat in the Devil's Eyeball. She hadn't made a fool out of herself, or proved what an old lady she was, until now.

On the riverbank, the group was laughing.

"Way to go, ballerina!" Stacey yelled.

What the hell. There was no place she could slink off to and recover her dignity. Gail turned toward the beach. Leaning on her paddle, she bowed low. "Grace is my middle name." It actually was.

Water dribbled from her flattened hair. Something green slithered from the shoulder of her life vest back into the water.

They all clapped and hooted. Laughing, Leon waded out to help her extract her boots from the mud and climb up the bank. After she'd shucked off her boots and rubber overalls and life vest, she found her beige pants and shirt so thin and clingy that her pink bra and panties positively glowed through the wet cloth. The river guide handed her a towel, which she quickly rubbed over her hair and then wrapped around her torso.

Leon patted a boat cushion on the sand beside him, and she sank down onto it gratefully, hoping to fade from the group's attention. Stacey picked up one of the jackets lying in a pile on the shore and draped it around Gail's shoulders. "Hey, Gail Grace, since you are clearly a water baby, I think you need to come diving with us in a couple of months."

Gail sarcastically responded, "Right." Then when nobody offered a follow-up retort, she asked, "Diving?"

"A bunch of us are going down to Roatan to a scuba resort for Christmas," Leon explained.

Leon's job was enough of a risk—fighting fires, rescuing people from all sorts of dire situations. His friends rafted wild rivers, and they were all scuba divers, too? It all sounded bold, maybe even awe-inspiring. But also life-threatening.

Combing her fingers through her wet hair, Gail smiled stiffly. "I don't even know where Roatan is."

"It's an island in the Caribbean, part of Honduras," the other John told her.

"It's great; you should come," Conrad said. "Palm trees, iguanas, hammocks swinging in the breeze. Warm water. Green morays, giant groupers, lobsters; clouds of fish of every conceivable color . . ." His voice took on a rhapsodic tone.

Roatan did sound great. But she had the flower shop to run, and then there were all Elisa's problems at Langston Green. She couldn't leave her daughter now. "I'm not a scuba diver," she told them all. Not to mention that Leon hadn't invited her.

He threw an arm around her. "You could be by Christmas."

Leon wanted her to come, then. That thought warmed her from the inside out. "Glad you think so," she said vaguely.

She'd always loved to swim. Nature shows featuring playful dolphins and goggle-eyed fish with weird lures on their heads had always fascinated her. Jacques Cousteau and his sons had been her heroes when she was a child. But didn't a member of their dive team die on one of their expeditions?

And didn't she hear stories all the time of divers dying out in the cold waters of Puget Sound?

Then there was Shark Week, which seemed to be featured at least four times a year on television. Scuba didn't sound like a hobby that any sane, fifty-something woman should suddenly take up.

Her hair and clothes gradually dried as they sat in the sunlit sand on the shore where the rafting company had set up a barbeque; hot dogs and baked beans and chips and cookies. There was soda and beer and a lot of joking around. The firefighters included the guide and her in their joshing as if they'd been part of the group forever.

Terry Langston had been her best friend for nearly twenty-three years. In fact, he'd been her whole world. They'd socialized with clients from Langston Green and on occasion, a few of his Peace Corps buddies. Now that Terry was gone, so were they.

This fire station crew all seemed so fearless. Stacey and April were confident, unmarried women. If only she was twenty or thirty years younger, she'd model herself after them, lift weights and run marathons and learn to fight fires.

April stole a swig from Leon's beer. Stacey teased Conrad about how his hair wouldn't stay in place on top of his bald spot. He laughed and swirled it into a curlicue on top of his head.

They were all so relaxed, so casual together. Leon was most likely the oldest, but nobody seemed to care about age or looks or anything but enjoying the day. She wanted to be part of this, be a member of Leon's tribe.

And then she realized that, damn it, she was doing it all again, hoping a man would create an entire social universe for her.

Just to have it all collapse when he vanished.

Chapter 8

The purple-haired woman standing before the counter in Gail's Flowers flipped through the display book. The frown on her face seemed to deepen with each new flower arrangement she studied. Finally, she closed the book and shoved it toward Gail.

"I'll have to think about it. These arrangements are all stunning, but they're so much more expensive than—"

Trader Joe's.

Gail could have sung the last two words in chorus with the noncustomer. The woman even turned her head in the direction of the offending establishment as she said it.

Gail made an effort to relax her jaw. "Thank you for coming in. We hope you'll stop by aga—" The ding of the bell over the door drowned out the end of her polite cliché as the older woman exited.

"Damn it!" She was not a woman prone to swearing out loud, but half a dozen choice obscenities flashed through her mind as she watched the woman stroll toward the competition.

As she had done for the last fourteen years, Gail dutifully went to her shop five days a week; they were closed Sundays and Mondays. But eighteen months ago, the opening of a Trader Joe's store only a half block away had slowed her florist business to a trickle. These days, customers were few. Only a handful of people stopped by each week to send long-distance birthday bouquets or anniversary arrangements. She didn't even have the pleasure of crafting those bouquets, merely passing each order along to the network florist closest to the gift recipient.

Terry had been so sure that leaving Gail and Charlie their respective florist shops in his will would guarantee incomes for his wife and daughter. He'd be crushed to know his expectations had been wrong. This month, the intake from Gail's Flowers was not even going to match the building lease payment. She doubted that she could sell the business, either; who in their right mind would buy a sinking ship? Her only recourse seemed to be to declare defeat, lock the door, and walk away.

Ever since breakfast, Gail's emotions had wavered between sadness and anger, all because of the dream she'd had last night. She'd been lost in a dense jungle, but one filled with roses and daisies and carnations, flowers that didn't belong in the tropics. From time to time she'd glimpsed a man who looked like Terry wandering through the trees ahead, but she could never catch up to him. She'd awoken with tears on her cheeks, a headache from clenching her jaw, and confusion about the message her brain—or the universe—was trying to send her. She'd lost Terry, that much was obvious. But in the dream, she was also lost among the flowers. Did that mean that it was time for her to find a way out?

She wanted to do her part to grow the family businesses. So far, Elisa had rejected all her offers to help at Langston Green. Terry's daughter had definitely inherited her father's stubbornness. She was determined to succeed on her own, even with her leg in a cast.

Gail had been an elementary teacher before becoming a florist; could she go back to that? But regaining her teaching certificate could take months, maybe even years. In the decades since she'd taught, there'd been all sorts of developments in public education: new math methods, mainstreaming of students with learning issues or physical challenges, and who knew what else? And after she got her certificate renewed, she'd have to compete for jobs with perky twentysomethings just out of college.

She sighed and drummed her fingers on the counter. Were all florists in this downward spiral? Hoping for sympathy, she called Charlene's Flowers in Woodinville.

"Hi, Mom," her daughter answered. "What's up?"

"How have your sales been recently?"

"A little slow. Only five arrangements so far this morning, but I've got a wedding planner showing up anytime now, so I'm hoping for a sweet deal there."

Wedding planners. Gail made a mental note to reach out to them.

"You doing okay in Seattle?" Charlie asked.

"Oh, everything's swell," Gail said. A ding at the other end of the line sounded like a period ending her comment.

"Gotta go, Mom; that client I was expecting just walked in. Hang in there. Love you."

"I love y—" She was talking to the dial tone.

Apparently, her woe-is-me event was going to be a solo gathering.

Three days had passed since the rafting trip. Leon hadn't called. But why should he? He clearly had lots of friends; he had a worthwhile job to go to. He was probably out with Jon right now, delivering premature quadruplets or giving lifesaving CPR to a heart-attack victim. While she was standing alone in an empty flower shop where the petals of the overstocked roses were curling with age.

She wanted to be dancing, to be back floating down the river, to be working with a team. *Damn.* She wanted Leon's life. At the same time, she missed her old life with Terry, the comfort of knowing a loving man was waiting for her at home in their comfortable house, planning dinner tonight and talking about what tomorrow would bring. She felt stuck between two worlds with no clear path to the future.

Suck it up, she ordered herself. She cleaned every square inch of the shop, polished the glass doors on the displays, even mopped the floors. She set aside sun-bleached ribbons and wrapping papers to donate to Goodwill. She speculated on future orders for Thanksgiving and Christmas inventory she most likely would not need. She checked the phone and the website to make sure they were both functional.

In the early afternoon, an order came in from a funeral home. Two standard arrangements, huge expensive fans of lilies and gladiolas and ferns with white satin sashes that said, ALWAYS IN OUR MEMORIES. One, she was told, was for the family of a teen who had died in a car wreck; the other for the funeral of a grandmother, ninety-seven years old. At least showy bouquets for funerals were not sold at Trader Joe's.

As she assembled the traditional funeral bouquets shown in the order book, the cloying sweetness of those standard arrangements increasingly irritated her. Her house had been filled with similar huge sprays of lilies and glads after Terry's death. Too much white and black, and purple and blue.

When did people start sending flowers to the bereaved, anyway? What was *that* supposed to mean? Ashes would be more appropriate. A lump of coal. Or maybe simply send an empty box; now *that* would be appropriately symbolic. She jabbed a required spray of nearly black gladiolas into the arrangement.

Death was never beautiful. It was bitter. It was lonely.

Flowers were still alive. Although their lives might be short, living things should be reserved for celebrations, but this somber bouquet did not look like a celebration of any kind. She carefully positioned three white calla lilies to match the photo in the order book. Had the original designer of this arrangement meant for these to stand for the Holy Trinity, or were they just supposed to add balance? Why were funeral arrangements always so monochrome and so similar? Anyone could tell someone had died just by looking at them, but the bouquets had no personality. Everyone's life should be memorialized, but not with some meaningless representation that could stand for *anyone's* existence.

After the delivery service picked up the finished bouquets, she set about making an appropriate bouquet for Terry. Ditching the typical crystal vase, she chose a tall ceramic pot with swirls of black and gold. She picked up one of the black gladiolas because Terry was gone, after all, and he'd left a black hole behind.

She wanted a celebration of life, she reminded herself. Her husband had loved color.

"It's nearly Harvest Fest, Terry," she told the gladiola. "We'll miss you there." To celebrate the memory of his favorite event, she added burnt orange and gold chrysanthemums, along with dried cattails and fern fronds. For the surviving family members Terry Langston had left behind, she added three of her prettiest roses, pale cream at the centers with pink and yellow tinges along the curled petals.

"Charlie," she murmured as she placed the first rose.

"Elisa."

"Me."

The arrangement still didn't feel quite right. It was a different sort of bouquet, all right, but it still lacked personality. She didn't even bother to flip the BE RIGHT BACK sign on the front door when she left and walked to the toy store a couple of doors down the street. There, she found what she was looking for. A small painted statue of a farmer with a hoe in hand, because Terry had spent most of his time in the fields at Langston Green. And a tiny toy backhoe, because like Elisa, he loved to drive that machine at the nursery.

Back in the shop, she glued the toys to long sticks and then positioned them among the flowers, along with his photo, borrowed from her purse. *There.* She stood back to view the finished product. *That* was a personal tribute to Terry, and she wished now she'd created such a bouquet for his memorial service. He'd been so popular in their community; so many people had come on that sad day. Were she to pass away, she doubted that more than a handful of those same people would attend for her, but most of them would be there out of respect for Terry, not because they were her friends.

The dream continued to haunt her. Seeing Terry in that flower jungle, always just beyond her reach. She bit her lip. *Get a grip, Gail Grace Langston. Are you going to be this pathetic the rest of your life?* She set the arrangement at the end of the front counter, where it wouldn't disturb customers too much but she could still see it.

Around three o'clock, a middle-aged man with a neatly trimmed moustache walked into the shop. Finally, another human being, in the flesh.

She leaned eagerly on the countertop. "Good afternoon. How can I help you?"

He shook his head. "Just browsing."

"Looking for flowers for a particular event? We have a book organized by holidays and special occasions." She pointed to the catalog on the counter.

"Anniversary," he muttered. He flipped a few pages, shoved his hands into his pockets, and moved to the cold case, staring at the flowers inside. "Roses are so . . ." His words trailed away.

"Romantic?" she prompted.

"Maybe. But also, so . . ." Frowning slightly, he looked away from the case, surveying her whole shop.

"Common? Expected?"

He chuckled, and a grin transformed his face. "I was going to say trite, but that sounds insulting."

She smiled back. "Traditional would probably be a better word."

"My wife is not exactly a traditional woman." He pointed to the bouquet Gail had crafted for Terry. "Now *that* arrangement has personality."

Pulling a wallet from his pocket, he extracted a photo and handed it to Gail. "Could you make something just for her?"

Although the woman in the picture had luxurious, thick wavy hair and huge dark eyes, she was not beautiful, or even pretty. She was middle-aged and wore an old-fashioned red tracksuit with white stripes along the front zipper of the jacket. But her mischievous facial expression and her surroundings immediately drew attention. Gail had a strange feeling that she'd met her somewhere before.

The woman was seated in a wheelchair, which had been pushed back from an easel holding a half-finished abstract. A smear of burgundy paint decorated the woman's cheek. A black toy poodle sat in her lap, grinning with typical doggie enthusiasm, eyes bright and mouth slightly open, as if about to bark at the camera. Behind the dog's head, the woman was making devil's horns with upturned fingers.

"I see what you mean," Gail said. "Let me think."

Rummaging around in her cabinets, she extracted a ceramic vase in the shape of a cart and plunked it on the counter between them. "Wheels for a lady who rolls through life."

They both stared. The black wheels weren't bad, but the pink and yellow flowers and the pale-blue ribbon painted on the little white cart were something out of a nursery rhyme. The thing looked like a lamb should be pulling it. When had she acquired all these sappy accoutrements in her store?

"No, that's just wrong." Grabbing the cart vase, she turned away from the counter. "Give me just a minute."

Grabbing up her can of spray glue, she bathed the ceramic cart, ripped crimson and gold foil into a variety of shapes, and slapped them onto the cart in a random pattern.

When she placed it on the counter this time, he said, "Ah. Better."

"Now, Mr. . . ."

"Gary."

"Gary, pick out some flowers that look like your wife."

"Jeannie."

"Like Jeannie. I'll be right back." Gary didn't look like the type to empty the cash register while she was gone, and he'd be sorely disappointed with the meager change there if he did. She walked back to the toy store and purchased two long-handled paintbrushes in different sizes, along with a tiny stuffed poodle.

When she returned to the shop, Gary had chosen red carnations, a spray of dark purple orchids, and several dried lotus pods. She arranged his selections, glued the dog toy onto a stick, stuck it and the paintbrushes and lotus pods into strategic positions, and stood back. It was definitely a unique arrangement.

"I love it!" he crowed. "Just one thing more." He pointed to Terry's bouquet. "Those roses symbolize someone, right?"

It threatened to bring tears to her eyes again, how this stranger could recognize the symbolism. "Me and my two daughters."

"I want two sunflowers for me and Jeannie."

She positioned the bright yellow flowers close together, counterbalancing the paintbrushes on the other side of the orchid sprays.

Gary grinned. "Now *that* is Jeannie. I can't wait to give it to her."

He took a photo of the bouquet with his phone. "I'll send this to you, too. You should put it up in here somewhere." He shifted his gaze meaningfully to the photos of traditional flower arrangements on the walls.

"I will," she promised. Taking his credit card, she charged

him only 10 percent above the cost of the flowers and toys.

"Too little." He scribbled another fifteen dollars in the "Tip" section of the credit card slip. "Jeannie says that artists need to charge for time and talent." Then he held out his hand. "You made my day, Missus . . ."

"Gail. Gail Langston." She shook his hand gratefully. "No, you made mine, Gary. Bring Jeannie in sometime, would you?"

"You bet." With a wink, he was gone.

A half hour later, another customer walked in. Gary Caber had been her good luck charm; business seemed to be picking up.

The redhead thumbed through her book, gazed at Gail and then at the refrigerator case, and then looked back to Gail. She seemed jittery. "Red roses are for passion, right?"

"That's one of the traditional interpretations," Gail said diplomatically.

"Then that's what I need, because that's what this guy and I have." The woman turned and struck a dramatic pose against the front of the counter. "Passion."

"A traditional dozen?" With a polite smile fixed on her face, Gail pulled twelve red roses from the case.

The woman straightened and chattered on. "He's a fireman."

"I met the crew at my local fire station," Gail commented. "They all seem like nice people. There were women, too."

"My man is not just a fireman," the woman told her. "He's also an EMT. He knows how to light my fire *and* check for smoke damage, if you know what I mean." She leaned on the counter again, thrusting her abundant breasts in Gail's direction and giving her a smoldering glance.

Gail lowered her gaze and focused on wrapping the paper around the flowers. Was this woman so effusive with every stranger she met?

The redhead continued with, "He calls me day and night.

We're debating about when to set the wedding date."

"That must be wonderful." Gail rang up the purchase. "I'm happy for you both."

After the woman walked out the door, Gail stared at the credit card receipt. A. K. Strand, Kirkland. What a strange, coincidental encounter. Not only did Gail Langston and A. K. Strand both know men who worked for fire departments, but their fire department friends were also emergency medical technicians.

She reminded herself that there were thousands of firefighters in Washington State, and probably half of them were also EMTs. Many women were attracted to firefighters; you only had to look at the covers of romance novels to see that. And she and Charlie had proven that the Langston women were not immune to the allure of men in blue uniforms.

Her memory played back Leon's words from their date and from the fire station before that.

Nobody you need to worry about.

Don't let her in here again.

Was Gail Langston only one of many women Leon was stringing along? Did all firemen have dozens of women chasing them?

She'd already invited Leon to the Harvest Fest party at Langston Green. Should she retract the invitation?

Chapter 9

The next day, she received the photo that Gary Caber had promised. Her personalized bouquet, the one she'd created for his wife. He included a photo of Jeannie holding the arrangement, her expression clearly delighted.

Jeannie had shoulder-length dark hair threaded with silver streaks. She looked to be approximately Gail's age, fiftyish. The more Gail looked at the photo, the more familiar Jeannie Caber looked. Screwing up her courage, Gail called the number she found at 411.com. A woman answered.

"Is this Jeannie Caber?"

"Yep. And I'm betting this is Gail Langston."

The wonders of caller ID. Gail hesitated a second, wondering what to say. *I need a friend and you look like you could be one?* She finally settled for, "Jeannie, I'd like to meet you someday."

"You already have. Decades ago. At high school in Tacoma. You used to be Gail Tomason, right?"

Gail was taken aback. "That sounds so strange now. That was two name changes ago. I thought you looked familiar."

"I used to be Jeannette Winkowski, the loudmouthed cheerleader. You were the artistic type."

Gail was surprised that Jeannie/Jeannette remembered her at all, let alone knew that she was artistic. "I only made posters and such."

"And you were on the swim team."

"Wow, I can't believe you remember that!" Gail had nearly

forgotten that year herself. She had never been a star, but she'd competed in short sprints and relay races. The scent of chlorine filled her imagination now.

"Get yourself over here." The woman rattled off her address. The house was only a few blocks away. "I'm dying to catch up with the artist who made this fantastic bouquet for me."

"I'm hardly an artist," Gail protested.

"This flower arrangement proves otherwise. Gary left this morning on an overnight business trip, so I could use some company. I have homemade soup and fresh bread. And I just pulled some brownies out of the oven."

Gail pressed her lips together to keep from drooling on the countertop. "I'm alone in my flower shop right now." She watched several people stroll by on the street. "I don't close for another hour."

"Expecting a mad rush of customers?"

Gail had to stop herself from making an unladylike noise. "*That* would be a change." She drummed her fingertips on the countertop for a beat, considering. "Oh, what the heck." She reached for the CLOSED sign. "I'll be there in ten minutes."

It took her fifteen, because parking was tight in Jeannie's neighborhood. The front door of the little red brick house was painted to look like the arch of a garden gate beckoning the guest into a world of flowers and ferns. Gail had to look hard to find the doorbell in the head of a butterfly.

The chime was answered by a shout of "Come in!" accented by the sharp yips of a small dog.

In the front room, the floor was bare beige tiles, punctuated by sparse black leather Danish furniture pushed against the walls. The walls were covered, floor to ceiling, with paintings of every conceivable subject. It was a riot of color. The air was filled with competing scents of oregano, basil, and cocoa.

A black toy poodle trotted to her, sniffed her shoes, then

emitted a shrill bark.

"Bring her in here, Ralph," a voice commanded from a doorway framed with turquoise trim. The dog turned and trotted in that direction.

Jeannie Caber looked just like the photo Gary had showed her, except that today she wore a blue tracksuit and had a streak of yellow on her chin. The cheerleader Gail remembered had always had the perfect expensive haircut, a shiny chin-length bob that all the other girls had envied. This woman's wild hair was twisted back into a bun, secured with a pencil. She sat in front of a canvas half-filled with purple, red, and yellow swirls.

The bouquet held center stage on a table against the far wall. But Jeannie's painting on the easel looked nothing like the flower arrangement.

"I'm painting how those flowers feel," she explained. "I'm going to call it 'Joyous.'"

"I'm so glad you like my arrangement."

"You'd have to be psychotic not to." Jeannie pointed a paintbrush at a nearby chair. "Sit."

On the table beside the chair lay the yearbook from their senior year at Tacoma High School. "Oh, now *there's* a stroll down Memory Lane." Gail pointed to the book. "I lost mine long ago."

"I confess, I cheated and looked you up yesterday after Gary told me about you." Jeannie leaned over the side of her wheelchair, snatched a small stretched canvas from a stack against the wall, and thrust it at Gail. "Grab one of those easels and paint."

"Oh, I don't—" Gail began.

"Have hands? Eyes?"

Those words rendered Gail speechless for a moment as she tried to recall what she'd intended to say. "I haven't painted since I was a teenager."

Before she had given birth to Charlie. Before Keith, Mark, and Terry. Before Elisa and Langston Green and the flower shop. So long ago.

"Take one of those disposable palettes and use whatever colors appeal to you." Jeannie indicated a stack of supplies and paint tubes on the table next to the bouquet. "And then paint what you want. Paint a happy memory. Paint how it feels."

Gail decided to paint her most recent happy memory: the float trip with Leon and the crew of Station 11. She started off by interspersing dabs of green and blue and lemon yellow for the river dapples, all the while wondering what she was supposed to say to this woman who knew her only as a teenager and a florist.

"I was paralyzed from the waist down in a drive-by shooting," Jeannie abruptly volunteered.

"My God." Gail stopped, mid–paint stroke. "I'm so sorry; I wasn't going to—"

Jeannie waved her paintbrush in the air. "Oh, please; everyone wants to know."

"Is the shooter in prison?"

"Never even identified him. Or her. It was a gang thing. I was just in the wrong place at the wrong time."

"That's horrible."

"Hey, shit happens." Jeannie shrugged. "But who wants to live in the past? I like to think of it as a wake-up call."

"For what? Gun control?"

Jeannie laughed out loud. "Good one, girlfriend! Yes, that, too, but it was a more personal jolt. It taught me that if you don't try your best to enjoy every day, you might as well be dead." She eyed a paint-splattered clock on the wall. "Fifteen minutes until the bread is done for dinner. Think you can finish by then?"

"Sure." Gail studied her canvas. "It's going to look like crap anyway."

"Looks like a happy day on the water to me. I love that bright splash of white in the upper right corner. But what's with the darkness in the lower left?"

And that's when Gail found herself telling her new friend all about Terry. And then all about Leon and the dancing at The Bayou and the rafting trip.

"The firefighters were all so"—Gail searched for the right word—"capable. Even the women. Especially the women. They all acted like they could do anything. And they seemed to assume I could, too." She swished a curl of aqua paint onto the canvas.

"Leon even suggested that I should learn to scuba dive," she finished. "How's that for a crazy notion?"

"He sounds like a catch," Jeannie remarked.

"He's fun, but I'm not so sure about him." She told Jeannie about overhearing the other firefighters mention a woman named Karma.

Jeannie's right shoulder raised and then dropped. "So he has a past. What difference does it make? You said you didn't want to get married again."

"I don't." Gail wasn't about to mention the curse.

"Then why not have fun? What do you have to lose? Hell, I'd go scuba diving with a hot firefighter if I could."

When Gail returned to her car, she found the side mirror on the driver's side lying in the street next to the front tire. How could any driver pass so close as to knock that off? The perpetrator hadn't even left a note on the windshield. The side of the Lexus was, thankfully, unscathed. She knelt and picked up the mirror, then opened her door and slid in, trying to remember the amount of her insurance deductible. Ah, well, as Jeannie would say, shit happens.

She started the engine, checked the rearview mirror and

looked over her left shoulder before pulling away from the curb. As she slid the car out of the parking spot, she spied an object on the sidewalk, and at the same time registered that the passenger side mirror was missing, too. *Damn it!*

She backed again into the parking space, got out, and picked up the second mirror. Shit might simply happen once in a while, but this was deliberate vandalism.

She surveyed the other cars on the street. All intact. Why just hers? Someone from the neighborhood, angry that a stranger was occupying a valuable space? Most of the parked cars were cheaper models than her Lexus. Could someone be angry about that? She'd have to ask Jeannie the next time she talked to her.

Elisa had been having problems with vandalism at Langston Green: broken irrigation pipes, destroyed plants, sand in the tank of the backhoe. Culminating in arson. Or at least it looked as if the burning of the old homestead had been intentional. Gail sucked in a breath. Had the nursery's Gremlin now switched his target to *her*?

"Don't be ridiculous," she scolded herself out loud. The vandal was in Woodinville, and here she was, nearly thirty miles away in Seattle. The Gremlin probably didn't even know Gail was associated with the Langston Green nursery. Her mirror-hating vandal was probably a local teenager on a dare, or something like that. That thought brought to mind the missing teenager Elisa was troubled about, her Hispanic employee, Timo Martinez.

A wave of guilt washed over Gail. She should be home right now, doing something useful to solve the family problems.

When Gail arrived back at her house, her daughters were in the kitchen. She was surprised to see both there, because always-independent Elisa had moved back to the nursery and was living in a camper while she waited for the insurance money to kick in to rebuild her office and apartment.

Charlie was trying to convince Elisa that she should buy a whole new wardrobe now that she'd finally gotten the cast off her leg, and just in time for the Harvest Fest party, too. Elisa was predictably arguing that new clothes were a waste of money.

"I work in a nursery, remember?" she argued, tossing her long dark hair. "I don't need fancy clothes. I can find what I need in the local thrift stores."

Charlie made a rude sound, retorting, "If you want to look like a bag lady. What about Jake? He'd like to see you in something other than dirty jeans and sweatshirts."

So the insurance investigator was now "Jake." Gail hoped he genuinely cared for Elisa and was not getting close just to pump her daughter for incriminating information.

"My jeans are not dirty," Elisa protested to her sister. "Except when I've been digging in the fields or moving inventory around."

"I rest my case." Charlie turned to Gail. "Where have you been, Mom? You didn't call or anything. We brought a pizza to surprise you."

Gail regarded the bare tabletop.

"We ate it," Elisa confessed.

Chuckling, Gail said, "Thanks for the thought, anyway. I didn't know I needed to check in. Charlie, I'm surprised you're not out with Jon."

"He's working a three-day shift at the station. They stay there round the clock, you know. He won't be off until day after tomorrow."

Which also might explain why Leon hadn't contacted her. Gail wanted to kick herself. She set the canvas on the countertop beneath a kitchen cabinet, leaning it against the wall. The paint—still damp—reflected the light from the ceiling fixture.

Gail was pleased at how well the painting had turned out. As Jeannie had said, the result had movement, from dark to light, from stillness to dancing sparkles.

Charlie said to her sister. "Now she's taken up *painting*."

Did her daughter sound sarcastic?

Elisa stood up and stepped back to admire the painting from a distance. "I had no idea you were so artistic, Mom. It reminds me of a sparkling stream."

Gail squeezed her stepdaughter's shoulder, delighted. "That's so perceptive, Elisa!"

"But wait, there's more!" Charlie sounded like a TV commercial. She rolled her eyes for emphasis, then leaned forward and said, "Mom floated down a river with Leon. She dances now, too. With Leon. At The Bayou. I caught 'em in the parking lot. She was barefoot, no less, and holding hands with him."

After shooting a scowl sideways at Charlie, Elisa plopped back into her chair. "I think that's wonderful, Mom."

Charlie sounded disapproving. Elisa sounded supportive, but surprised.

Gail's eyes darted involuntarily to the family portraits on the dining room wall. One photo—taken before she'd come into Terry's life—was of Elisa and Terry and Elisa's birth mother, Maria Elena, a petite, fiery Mayan woman. How often had Gail held her tongue while little-girl Elisa compared her stepmother to the exotic, adventurous behavior of her birth mother, who wore bright colors and played the Andean flute and chased butterflies? Once, in a fit of anger, teenage Elisa had described the Langston clan as "beige."

It was an adjective that Gail found disturbingly accurate. But beige Gail and Charlie and Terry had stuck by Elisa's side, while colorful Maria Elena had flitted back to exotic Guatemala.

"I did have a life before you two came along," Gail told

them. "I used to paint. I also used to dance all the time with your father, Charlie. As a matter of fact, Keith and I met on a dance floor."

Charlie raised a well-groomed eyebrow. "You never told me anything about dancing, Mom. Or painting."

Gail pursed her lips. What had living with all her memories of grief over Keith and Mark done to her daughter Charlene? Had she always been a cautious, solemn, boring mother, even while she was married to Terry?

As she gazed at the two young women she'd raised, Gail wanted to ask them whether she'd ever been fun. But she was afraid of what their answers might be. Instead, she said, "You have no idea what I might do next."

I just might take up scuba diving.

Charlie glanced at Elisa and made a spiraling, I-think-she's-going-crazy motion with her hand.

Elisa frowned at her sister. "I think it's about time."

Chapter 10

Before lunchtime the next day, Gail was again bored out of her mind in her florist shop. Was this what the rest of her life was going to be like, dutifully keeping the business hours posted on the door, waiting in her empty shop for customers to drop in? This was ridiculous. For decades, she'd made decisions based on other people's schedules. Charlie's, Elisa's, Terry's. But she no longer could pretend that her plans were based on taking care of another person. Whatever decisions she made, the consequences would be hers alone. Did that make her rudderless, or free?

Gail used the shop computer to compile a list of wedding planners. She emailed them all, offering 10 percent off any order over a hundred dollars. *There, done.* What next? She still had two hours to go before closing.

Jeannie's words echoed in her head. "Hell, I'd go scuba diving with a hot fireman if I could."

Her friend might not be able to scuba dive, but Gail Langston could. She called the closest scuba store and asked about classes for beginners.

"If you can start tonight, you're in luck," the owner said. "We have a six-week course that begins at 6:30. One hour of classroom instruction, and then an hour in the pool."

She hesitated. She didn't have a swimsuit with her; she'd bought a chicken to cook for tonight's dinner.

Which she would eat alone, unless Charlie came home to join her.

Leon's words rang through her imagination: "You could be a scuba diver by Christmas." Then Jeannie's: "Why not have fun?"

Why not, indeed? She could buy a swimsuit after work. The chicken could keep until tomorrow. She could roast it and invite Leon over for dinner.

"Sign me up," she told the dive shop owner.

It was nearly October. What store would have swimsuits for sale? She'd have to sort through the racks at Value Village and hope that a used suit would fit her slender frame. She was almost ready to hang out the CLOSED sign and drive over there when the first customer of the day entered the shop.

Gail thrust the order book in her direction, but the woman waved the binder of photos away. "I'm looking for customized. Jeannie sent me."

Her daughter was having a baby. Tomorrow, by scheduled C-section. The daughter was thirty-five.

"Melinda isn't married," the woman volunteered. "And she's a little anxious about parenthood. But she desperately wants a baby. She's having a girl."

"Congratulations." Clearly, both mother and daughter had guts. Gail swept her hand around the shop. "Pick out some flowers that remind you of your daughter, and then choose a few to represent your new granddaughter. I'll go look for an appropriate vase."

She found one on a back shelf, sturdy but feminine, pale green with rose and white swirls. She and the customer went to the toy shop together and picked out a tiny teddy bear and a fairy with gossamer wings, and the woman applauded Gail when the arrangement—pink and white calla lilies, daisies, ferns, and the toys on sticks among delicate baby's breath— was complete.

"It's perfect," the customer crowed. "And it's personal. I could pick up a bunch of flowers at Trader Joe's, but I couldn't get *this* arrangement anywhere but here. Jeannie's right; you are an artist."

"Would you mind if I took a photo and hung it on my wall?" Gail asked.

"I'd be honored. In fact, that's a great idea." The customer used her cell phone to take her own photo while Gail snapped a couple of shots.

Gail's smile lasted long after the woman left the shop. Take that, Trader Joe's! She hung out the Be Right Back sign and walked down the block to the toy store and bought a selection of small toys that could fit into bouquets the next time a referral of Jeannie's walked in. She sent the photos of Jeannie's and Melinda's bouquets to a photo-processing shop down the block to enlarge them for her walls. She might even be able to find frames for them at the thrift store, along with that swimsuit she needed.

The other eight students in the Beginning Scuba class looked to be in their twenties or early thirties. They had all come as couples or friends. As they introduced themselves, Gail felt like the awkward girl who'd arrived at the party late and without a date. She took some consolation from noticing that the instructor, Richard, was going gray at the temples. He promised that he would be her partner when it was time to do drills.

Drills? Even the word was intimidating.

The discussion of pressure changes in the water was fascinating, although she could tell that the math involved with dive tables would be a challenge; it had been decades since she'd studied anything. The written exam was not going to be easy to pass. As Richard lectured, she glanced at the other students around the table. None of them looked as anxious as she felt.

The first pool session turned out to be a swim challenge,

twenty laps. Gail was thrilled when she beat the rest of the class to the finish line. As she pulled herself out of the pool, the instructor high-fived her.

Charlie looked up from her laptop on the kitchen table as Gail entered. "Nice hairdo, Mom."

"Unintentional." Gail raised a hand to her damp hair. "I didn't have a blow dryer with me."

As Gail set her new mask, snorkel, and fins down on a chair, Charlie's mouth dropped open.

"You weren't kidding?" Her daughter raised an eyebrow. "First Leon and then dancing. And floating down rivers. And painting." Charlie glanced at the canvas now, still in the same place against the wall where Gail had left it last night. "And now snorkeling? Isn't it a little cold for that?"

Gail hesitated. Her daughter seemed unlikely to applaud the new challenge she'd taken on. "For now, I'm just swimming, Charlie." *And how was she going to explain the sudden urge to dive into a pool?* "When I ran into Linda the other day, we talked about going on a tropical vacation someday," she lied. "So I thought I'd practice first in the pool."

Charlie pursed her lips. "Wow, Mom. I'm not sure who you are anymore." Her daughter turned her head toward the back door. "Do you hear that?"

Gail turned that direction, too. "Hear what?"

"It sounded like a cat."

Opening the back door, Gail surveyed the empty backyard. She closed the door again. "No cat."

Taking a wine glass from the cabinet, she reached for the half-filled bottle of wine on the counter. She was no longer certain who she was, either, but she didn't like her daughter's disapproving tone. When Charlie moved back into the house after Terry's death, Gail had been grateful, but now she wasn't so sure she welcomed her daughter's judgmental company so often. She drew in a deep breath as she poured herself a glass of cabernet.

"I'm hardly ready for the grave, Charlene." Taking a sip from her glass, she rested her backside against the kitchen counter. "Once upon a time, back when dinosaurs roamed the earth, your father and I had a lot of exciting plans for future adventures."

"Really?" Charlie scooted her chair back from the table.

"Keith and I were going to learn to surf. We were going to ride motorcycles down the West Coast to the tip of Baja."

Charlie's face took on a doubtful expression as she pushed her honey-blond hair behind her ear with a manicured fingertip.

"I was barely nineteen when your father and I married." Gail took another sip, swirling the wine in her mouth as she tried to remember what it felt like to be that age.

"Huh," Charlie murmured softly, seeming chastised. Rising from her chair, she walked down the hall to her bedroom and then returned shortly with a framed photograph in hand. Keith Garrett, standing on the tarmac in his flight suit, his helmet tucked under one arm, his other hand on his helicopter. "This is the only way I think of him, Mom."

Gail's heart sank. "That's natural, sweetheart. You never knew him. But your father was a real person, not just a photograph. He was wonderful and kind. We thought we'd have a whole future of adventures. Our time together was much too short."

"And then there was Mark."

Gail winced. Had Charlie made that sound as if her mother was a loose woman picking up men on street corners, or was that all in her imagination? She sighed. "Mark and I talked about hiking the Pacific Crest Trail someday."

Charlie pressed her lips together for a minute, then she said in a mournful voice, "I barely remember him."

Gail swallowed, trying to dislodge the lump that formed in her throat.

"What did you and Dad plan for the future?"

Gail knew Charlie meant Terry Langston, the only father her daughter had ever known. She swallowed again, thinking about all the future events she and Terry had talked about. "Oh, enjoying grandchildren eventually."

Charlie's forehead creased. "Not going there. At least not right now."

"Visiting all the national parks. Touring Hawaii for our twenty-fifth anniversary—" Gail's voice broke at the last memory. Maybe none of their dreams had been earth-shattering, but she and Terry Langston had planned for a peaceful, sweet future. The note she had found pinned in her dress flashed into her brain. *What are we celebrating?*

Hot tears pooled in Gail's eyes, and she turned to set the wine glass down on the counter. Charlie had just reminded her that all the men she had loved had died horrific, lonely deaths. The odds against that happening to a suburban woman who did her best to live risk-free? Astronomical.

Charlie broke into her morbid thoughts, startling Gail with, "Did you see Jon and Leon on the news?"

"What?"

Shaking her head, Charlie thumbed her phone. "Of course you didn't. You were swimming. Look." She held out the phone as a tiny video began to play.

At first Gail saw only flames shooting from a burning apartment building as a newscaster was saying something about a heroic rescue of an elderly woman in a wheelchair. Peering closer, she noticed a ladder extending into a window and then a man in full turnouts with mask and tank appearing in the window frame. Stepping carefully to the ladder, he turned and held out his arms, and another man in similar gear slid a stretcher out the window onto the ladder. A figure was strapped onto the stretcher, and then the uppermost firefighter attached a strap from his harness to the top of the stretcher. Both firefighters paused to remove their masks, and Gail recognized Leon as the second man and Jon as the first. With Leon lowering the stretcher and Jon, below, controlling its descent, they began a slow crawl down the ladder. The video ended, and Charlie pulled her phone back.

Gail had one hand pressed against her chest. "I didn't realize that EMTs ever went into burning buildings."

"Pretty heroic, huh? Leon and Jon are full-fledged firefighters as well as EMTs, Mom. In most fire departments, they have to be."

Gail couldn't erase the image from her head of Leon emerging from the flames. She didn't want to think of him crawling through fire.

Her daughter stood up and wrapped her arms around her. "I'm sorry to give you a hard time about the dancing and rafting and painting, Mom. It's just, you know, I worry about you. I know you're not ancient, and you deserve to have fun sometimes. And Leon seems okay. Jon worships him."

Gail swallowed painfully. "Leon is a very nice man, and yes, we're having fun. But he's only a friend."

"That's good. Because . . ." Charlie hesitated for a breath, then picked up her cell phone again. "I wasn't sure whether I should tell you, but when I went to meet Jon yesterday, I saw Leon talking to a woman outside the station. They looked pretty intimate."

Charlie turned the phone toward Gail. The photo was in silhouette, but Gail could see that a long-haired woman had her face raised toward Leon and one hand resting on his forearm.

Gail's throat felt tight again. "We're not in an exclusive relationship," she told her daughter. "We're just getting to know each other."

The men who promised themselves to her always left her in horrible, dramatic ways. It was a good thing that Leon had other women. Yes, she would welcome some romance in her life. But she did not need romance with another adrenaline junkie. She was not looking for a permanent partnership with Leon Maxwell.

Chapter 11

Leon promised to bring the wine to Gail's house for dinner. After perusing the labels in the liquor aisle of the grocery store and selecting an Oregon pinot gris, he'd returned to his cart to find someone else's salmon filet in the basket.

Karma materialized out of the seafood section to slide her arm through his. "I thought we'd have fish for dinner tonight, babe." She flashed her best Cheshire Cat grin. "With rice pilaf and a green salad?"

"Did you follow me here?"

Pasting an injured look on her face, she flicked her hair back over her shoulder. "A girl has to shop, too, you know."

Leon picked up the package of fish and held it out to her. "You've got the wrong cart, lady. And the wrong man."

Her lips turned down in a pretty pout. "You can't still be mad at me, baby. Whatever you think I did, I'm sorry. Let's make up." Clinging to his arm, she lifted her face and planted a kiss on his lips.

Pressing the plastic-wrapped salmon to her chest, he gave her a gentle shove to break her hold on his arm. She stepped back, banging into the door of a freezer case, a shocked expression on her face. The packaged fish slapped down onto the floor.

A meat department employee, a middle-aged man in a stained apron stepped between them. His eyes squinted suspiciously at Leon before he turned toward Karma. "Are you all right, ma'am?"

She sniffed and rubbed her arm. The employee swiveled to face Leon, a dare on his face. "Is this man harassing you?"

Both Leon and Karma said "No" in the same breath. Then Karma tucked her chin and demurely said, "I'm sure my boyfriend didn't mean to hurt me."

"I'm not her boyfriend," Leon told the guy. Jerking his cart away, he pushed it rapidly down the aisle.

Women shoppers glared at him and shook their heads. "You should be ashamed of yourself," one hissed as he passed.

What could he do to make her stop? He had already told his apartment manager never to let Karma in again.

"I should have known better than to rent to another unmarried man," the manager had grumbled. "You're old enough to know that the 'Do 'em and dump 'em' method always comes back to bite you in the ass."

"You've got it wrong—" Leon had begun.

The manager had waved a hand to cut him off. "If the police start hanging around here, you're out, buddy." And then he'd closed the door in Leon's face.

A few days ago, Karma had brought flowers for him to the station. He threw away both the card and the bouquet.

She kept showing up at his apartment. At the fire station when he was on shift.

Now she was following him to the grocery store.

How the hell was he going to get rid of her? Would asking a judge to issue a restraining order make him the laughingstock of the community? Would any police officer enforce a no-contact order? Karma was a pro at forcing tears into her big brown eyes and a pretty pout onto her lips. She seemed determined to cling to him like a lamprey, no matter how often he told her he didn't want a relationship with her. He didn't want her, period.

He wanted Gail.

But if Karma knew that, she'd want Gail gone.

He drove a circuitous route to Gail's house. There was no sign of Karma's car in his rearview mirror. But he parked a few doors down from Gail's house, just to be sure.

Chapter 12

The roasted rosemary chicken, baked potatoes, and salad Gail fixed for Leon was simple, and she fretted that in no way could it match up to dinner at The Bayou. Over the meal, she and Leon talked about his recent EMT runs at the fire station and about how Elisa and her business partner, Gerald, were pulling together the first Harvest Fest since Terry's death. Because the main building had burned down, the party was to take place in the old homestead barn at the nursery.

"Elisa's a nervous wreck," Gail told Leon. "She's so worried that it won't live up to the neighborhood's expectations. Harvest Fest was Terry's big event every year."

"I remember." Leon put his hand over hers on the table.

"And she won't let me help out at the nursery in any way." She sighed.

"Elisa strikes me as pretty tough. She'll do fine. But is that guy still dogging her, that insurance investigator?"

"Jake Street," Gail reminded him. "Well, now it seems like he wants to romance Elisa instead of prosecuting her. I hope he's not just pretending to trick her into giving him information he could use against her."

"I hope not, too. Elisa's an intriguing young woman." Leon lifted another forkful of chicken from his plate. "She and Street started off with a strong connection: he did save her life."

"I thought you and Jon saved her life."

He shrugged. "Street called 911; otherwise we'd never have known she was lying out there in the field. He and Elisa would make an interesting couple."

Gail shook her head. "Elisa's not going for it. See, Street's not done with the investigation. Now he's focused on the missing employee, Timo Martinez. Timo's only a teenager. Elisa hasn't seen him since the day of the quake, when she gave him most of Langston Green's petty cash to hire some temp workers."

Leon's brow wrinkled. "Uh-oh."

"The worst part is that Elisa will never believe that Timo is guilty."

"A friend of hers, huh?"

"They look enough alike to be brother and sister. I think Timo reminds her of her birth mother." Gail pointed to the family photos on the wall.

Leon studied the array of photos for a minute, his gaze moving from the old photo of red-haired Terry and black-haired, dark-skinned Elisa and Maria Elena to the newer Langston family with blond Gail and Charlie. His gaze remained on Terry for a long time. In the photo, Terry had his arm wrapped around Gail. Was Leon comparing himself to her deceased husband?

She nervously fingered her necklace, thinking about the tiny photos of herself and Terry inside the locket.

"I'm confused," Leon finally admitted. "I thought Charlie was your biological daughter and Elisa was adopted."

"Charlie *is* my biological daughter, but not Terry's. Elisa is Terry's biological daughter, and Maria Elena's." She nodded again toward the photo. "They met in Guatemala when Terry was in the Peace Corps."

He continued to stare at the photos. "So ... Charlie's father?"

Naturally, he would wonder now. "Keith Garrett," she said. "I was a teenage bride."

He glanced at her, one eyebrow raised.

"I'll be right back." She pushed her chair from the table and strode to her bedroom, pulled the old framed wedding photo out of her bedside drawer, and then returned to the table and handed it to Leon. In the photo, Gail wore a white minidress and daisies in her hair; Keith was in dress uniform.

"Wow. You *were* just a kid," Leon said in amazement. "And he was a soldier?"

"I was nineteen. He was an army helicopter pilot."

He handed back the photo. "Does Charlie get to see him often?"

Gail's heart did a somersault. She clasped the photo to her chest. The heavy silver frame felt cold against the bare skin in the vee of her blouse. "Charlie has never seen him," she admitted sadly. "Keith died only a few months after our wedding."

"I'm so sorry, Gail. I should never have—"

"It's okay. It's my history." Should she tell him about Mark now? No, that was too much. She already felt as if they were treading water in a sea of tragedy. She forced a smile. "I don't regret a minute of it. And I couldn't imagine life without Charlie and Elisa." She laid the photo facedown on the empty chair next to her.

"You have a lot of memories to treasure."

"Yes," she admitted, again fondling the locket at her throat. "We had a great life. *I* had a great life."

"It's not over."

Gail hesitated, confused.

"Your life, Gail," he said, his clear gray-blue eyes boring into hers. "It's not over."

She folded her hands on the tabletop to cover her awkwardness. "Now I want to hear some of your memories, Leon."

"Mine?" He snorted. "A lot of crazy times with friends. No sweet, nostalgic, family-oriented ones like these. I hope those are yet to come." He gently caressed her hand with his fingers.

She smiled, squirming under the peculiar feeling that Keith was sitting on the chair next to her and Terry was watching from the wall. In the silence that fell, she heard the ticking of the clock in the living room, and was that a plaintive cry outside the back door? She listened but didn't hear the sound again. It must have been her imagination. Why was she hearing cats?

Leon seemed preoccupied, too. As she busied herself gathering up the dishes and preparing to serve the lemon cake she'd brought home from the bakery, his phone buzzed three times. He frowned each time he stared at it, and then he finally shut it off, apologizing as he slid it back into his pocket.

"Do you need to take that?" She placed a piece of lemon cake in front of him. "Are you on call?"

"No, and no. It's just a persistent salesperson," he responded, not looking at her. He picked up a fork. "This looks delicious."

"I don't want to keep you from anything important."

He picked up her hand. "You're not, Gail. I want to be here. I've been looking forward to this all day."

But when a loud bang sounded from the street out front, Leon rushed to the living room window and peered through the blinds.

"No worries. Your neighbor just dropped his trash can," he reported on returning to her side.

"Are you okay, Leon?"

His expression grew cautious. "Of course."

"You seem jumpy."

He ran his hand over his close-cropped hair. "Just nervous about behaving myself. The last time I was in your house, I stuck my foot in my mouth."

When she didn't respond immediately, he added, "With the story about the guy and the knothole."

She chuckled. "I remember."

"So we all know what *my* days are like," he said, changing the subject. "Tell me about yours. What do you do for excitement?"

Excitement? Her swallow of wine threatened to choke her, and she coughed for a second before she could answer. "I don't. Do anything for excitement, I mean. I haven't done anything except work and stay home for a long time."

Yeesh. Couldn't she have made up some interesting hobby or something? Leon's eyes would be glazing over any second now. She was even boring herself. She quickly added, "But I'm trying to branch out. Recently, I went dancing and river rafting with this handsome, fascinating man. I'd like to do more things like that."

He leaned in to give her a quick kiss on the lips.

She didn't tell him about scuba training. One, she hadn't done anything except listen to a lecture and pass a swimming test. Two, she was afraid she wouldn't make it all the way through the class. Three, she didn't want him to think she'd taken up the sport just for him. She wasn't sure how long she'd be dating Leon Maxwell. This was just for fun, she told herself, leaning in for another kiss.

His lips were soft and warm. When he pulled her from her chair into his lap, she didn't resist. His arms felt so strong, yet tender at the same time.

"Are you an artist?" He swiveled to glance through the doorway at the painting, which she'd propped up against a stack of books on the big table in the dining room. "Is that your painting? I love it."

"Really?"

"Really." His eyes were still fixed on it. Lovely, soft gray eyes with hints of blue. Which he now moved to focus on her. "It reminds me of a flowing river."

"I painted that a couple of days ago." She abruptly realized she wanted him to have it. "It's yours."

He grinned. "Are you sure?"

"If you really want it."

"Hell, yes, I want it!" He stood up, walked to the painting, and picked it up in his hands. "I'm going to hang it in my bedroom, where I can look at it before I go to sleep and see it first thing in the morning." After setting it down, he came back and kissed her again. "Thank you."

Then he looked at his watch and groaned. "Speaking of first thing in the morning, I'd better help you clean up, and then I should go. Our next shift starts tomorrow at six a.m."

"I don't need help." Gail moved their dessert plates to the sink. She'd been on the verge of inviting him to her bedroom. Charlie wasn't due home for hours, if at all. But now she felt a twinge of relief. No need to be bold tonight; she'd been daring enough by giving him the painting.

"Dinner was great," he said, putting his hands on both her shoulders. "And about Monday . . ."

He hadn't mentioned anything about Monday. She turned to face him. "What about it?"

A sly look settled on his face. "I know your shop is closed on Mondays. I'll pick you up at nine a.m."

She cocked her hip and frowned. "How do you know I'm not busy?"

His right eyebrow rose. "Are you?"

Should she make something up? She didn't want him to think she just sat around waiting for him.

"Nine a.m.," he repeated. "Wear clothes that you can ruin."

"What? Why would I ruin clothes? You're not taking me river rafting again, are you?"

His eyes sparkled. "No."

"And I'm not bungie-jumping. Ever."

He chuckled. "Duly noted."

"You're really not going to tell me what we're going to do?"

"Nine a.m. Monday." After giving her a swift kiss, he headed for the front door.

Chapter 13

"I thought we were going to paint again." Instead of the easels and canvasses Gail expected, Jeannie had covered a big table with plastic. The center of the table was dominated by a small mountain of clay.

"We are. Eventually." Jeannie rolled to the table. "But first we're going to make things to paint. I'm going to make a star, how about you?" She grabbed a handful of clay.

Gail was confused. "Are we making Christmas ornaments?"

Jeannie snorted. "You are such a dork." Picking up a long glass rod from a bunch inside a coffee mug, she pointed it at Gail. "You gave me the idea, with the toy dog and paint brushes in your bouquet." She glommed her ball of clay onto the end of the rod to demonstrate.

Gail laughed. Of course. Someone had to make those tiny objects in the toy shop. "Well, duh."

"Dork." Jeannie pulled the ball of clay from the rod and began to pinch it into a star shape.

"Dingbat," Gail retorted. She'd closed the shop early again to come, but the fun she had with Jeannie was well worth losing the sale of one or two bouquets. She pulled out a chair, grabbed a ball of clay, sat down, and stared at the lump on the table in front of her. What did she want to make?

Jeannie had her star completed in no time. Pressing it onto a rod, she waved it toward Gail like a fairy godmother. "Three wishes. First one: I wish you would tell me more about the fireman."

Gail raised an eyebrow. "Aren't *I* supposed to get the wishes?"

"Not in this house. Now spill. What have you been up to?"

She told Jeannie about scuba diving lessons and dinner with Leon.

Her friend sighed. "Ah, adventure *and* romance."

"Not exactly. I'm just having fun, like you suggested. But he's kind of secretive, and I don't know what to think about that. He keeps getting phone calls he won't answer, at least not when he's with me."

"And you've already told him everything about *your* life?"

"Uh . . . he already knew about Terry. And I told him about Keith."

"But not about Mark?"

Gail frowned. "Who are you, my therapist?"

Jeannie didn't reply, just leaned forward in her wheelchair and stared more forcefully into Gail's eyes as if she were trying to hypnotize her.

Gail cast her gaze down to the table. "I don't want him to think I'm a black widow or something worse."

A scoffing sound came out of Jeannie's mouth. "What could be worse?"

Gail couldn't help but chuckle at the idea of something worse than a serial killer. "A shit magnet?"

"What?"

Meeting her friend's gaze again, Gail shrugged. "That's Elisa's expression for someone who attracts trouble. I'll get around to telling Leon, I promise. Maybe on Monday. He has something mysterious planned, then. All he will tell me is that it might ruin my clothes."

"Interesting. A man of mystery. I can't wait to hear the next chapter in this romantic suspense novel." Jeannie eyed the winged creature Gail was creating. "Is that an angel?"

"A fairy." Gail held the figure out in her palm. "You gave me that idea with your wand." She studied it critically. "The wings are too heavy, though. A fairy should have gossamer wings."

"Agreed." Jeannie reached over and ripped off a wing.

"Hey! Stop maiming my fairy!"

Alarmed at Gail's tone, Ralph stood up from his dog bed on the floor and issued two sharp yips.

"Down, killer," Jeannie told him, then turned back to Gail. "Gossamer." She screwed up her face for a minute, thinking. "Netting and . . ."

Gail suggested, "Picture hanging wire?"

"Could do the job. I have both." Jeannie gestured with her chin to a cabinet. "Check the second and third drawers. You'll probably want the needle-nose pliers, too."

The tiny wire and net fairy wings were such a success that Gail went on to create wings for a dragonfly and a butterfly. Before attaching them, she studied the bodies she'd created. "Doesn't clay need to be fired?"

"Baking in the oven is fine," Jeannie said. "I googled it."

"Well, then, it must be true."

By the time Jeannie's husband, Gary, came home, she had created stars and half moons in multiple sizes, as well as several birds. Gail had fashioned two fairies, three dragonflies, and a couple of butterflies. The wings were detached; they'd have to find a way to glue them on after the clay was fired. She'd also created a tiny woman seated with a book in her hands.

"What's with the tiny lady?" Gary pointing to the human figure among the other creations they'd laid out on two cookie sheets.

Instead of being attached to a glass rod, the miniature clay woman had a tab of clay extending down from her backside. "She's an experiment," Gail explained. "Maybe she'll sit on the edge of a vase or pot."

He nodded. "Jeannie told me you were creative."

"I'm learning."

"Hell, I'm the one who's learning," Jeannie pulled a cookie sheet onto her lap. "Grab that other tray, Gary." She rolled toward the kitchen, telling her husband, "Dinner will have to be nuked. I'm baking fairies and librarians right now."

"That's my cue to leave." Gail stood and picked up her coat.

In the kitchen, Jeannie shut the oven door and then rolled back to peer at Gail through the doorway, a sly grin on her face. "Back to the hot fireman?"

"Not until Monday."

"Then we'll paint these tomorrow. One thirty?"

"I can't wait."

Gail let herself out and walked to her car, relieved to find it untouched this time. Replacing the side mirrors had cost a small fortune at the dealer. As she drove home, she smiled, planning the colors for her clay creations. They'd need glitter, too. And sequins. Maybe even a few tiny glass jewels. She'd stop at the crafts store tomorrow morning before work.

Jeannie was right, she *was* creative.

Chapter 14

After his three-day shift was over, Leon returned to his apartment. Karma had shown up at the station while he and Jon were out on a call, but thankfully, she'd left by the time they'd returned. He deleted the four voicemail messages she'd left him, along with the sixteen texts. The woman was relentless.

He scanned the parking lot carefully before walking to his door. No sign of her car, the little white Subaru. No sign of Karma herself.

His apartment seemed to be just as he'd left it. But then, as he emerged from the bathroom, he noticed Gail's painting on his bedroom wall. The beautiful blue-green canvas was now crisscrossed with ugly slashes.

"Shit, Karma! Goddamn it!" He stomped to the front door. He'd paid the manager to change the locks, how the hell had she gotten in? The lock seemed undamaged, as did the living room window that looked out on the second-floor landing. His office also bordered the landing, and when he inspected the window there, he found it closed, but not locked. The sill was dented with what looked like screwdriver marks. Crap, he had opened the window the day before he reported to the station. Obviously, he hadn't locked it before leaving his apartment. He pounded his fist against his thigh in frustration. "Shit, shit, shit!"

He sat on the bed for a long time, staring at the mutilated painting. There was no way he could repair it. Finally, he took it down from the wall and placed it in the closet so it wouldn't hurt every time he saw it.

Fingering his phone, he wondered whether he should call or text the bitch. No, that would only give her satisfaction, knowing she'd dealt him the blow she intended. He didn't find Karma's other gift until he peeled back the covers to get into bed. There was a red lipstick kiss imprint on his pillowcase, and a pink lace thong beneath the pillow. He snapped a photo with his phone before he ripped off the case and tossed both it and the thong into the trash.

How the hell was he going to get rid of Karma? All the information he'd found on dealing with stalkers recommended ignoring them or appealing to the court for a no-contact order if their behavior was threatening. *That* would be beyond humiliating. He could imagine the scene now, the judge asking why he, a mature, macho fire department EMT, needed protection from this beautiful young woman? Not to mention, what could he use as evidence of harassment? Karma could swiftly turn the tables on him, as she had in the grocery store. And a court report would be public record. His bosses could easily get their hands on it. Any sort of domestic dispute could easily be a black mark on his record.

His cell phone buzzed. A text from Gail. Still on for tomorrow?

9 am, old clothes, boots, he texted back.

No hints? she responded.

See you tomorrow, he replied, smiling. Thank God Karma hadn't yet discovered where Gail lived or worked.

Chapter 15

On Monday morning, Leon drove Gail to an overgrown corner lot on the outskirts of Seattle. The rusting structure for a swing set dominated the site, but the swings were long gone. Only a few feet of rusting chain dangled from the horizontal support pipe overhead. What might have been a slide at one time was now a twisted heap of metal next to a dilapidated fence. A discarded mattress and a tangle of books and clothes were mildewing among the weeds, and dented beer cans and cigarette butts littered the bald areas of dirt. A barrel in one corner looked as if it had been used as a fire pit.

This was not a neighborhood Gail would have chosen to spend time in. Four sketchy-looking adolescent boys clustered on the sidewalk a short distance away, sharing a joint. Marijuana was legal in Washington State now, but only for those over twenty-one, and not in public. Who was supervising these kids? If these boys got high this early in the morning, what did they do the rest of the day?

"We're here because?" she prompted Leon, who sat beside her in his RAV4.

"Wait for it," he said. "We're a few minutes early. Oh, and you'll need these." He twisted around, reached into a paper sack behind her seat, and then handed her a pair of gloves. Leather, size small, brand new.

A huge truck rumbled into position on the other side of the lot. The company name on the side had mostly weathered away, but she could still make out the word LANDSCAPING below that. A man and a woman climbed out of the cab.

Leon opened his door. "The cops are here."

"Cops?" Gail joined Leon on the sidewalk.

"Donovan Kelly, Marina Petrov," Leon introduced them, pointing. "Seattle Police. Guys, this is Gail. She volunteered to help today."

"I was shanghaied," she told them. "And I still don't know why."

Another SUV pulled up, and out spilled four of Leon's colleagues from the fire station: Jon, Stacey, April, and Conrad.

"Let's do this!" Stacey said, pounding one gloved fist into the palm of her other hand.

"Why would we do this?" Leon bellowed, startling Gail.

"Because we should!" they all chorused together.

April laughed at the confusion on Gail's face. "That's what we call ourselves, BecauseWeShould. There's a 'dot org' after that on our website. Firefighters and police officers doing occasional volunteer projects in our time off. Today, restoring this playground for the neighborhood kids."

Gail studied the area doubtfully. "Cleaning it up, maybe. But I don't see anything worth restoring."

"'Rebuilding' is probably more accurate," Marina corrected. "You'll see." She pointed to a variety of tools in the bed of the truck. "Choose your weapon."

Gail chose a rake.

Leon grabbed a sledgehammer. "Let's level this place!"

As he strode toward the abandoned swing set structure, the teenage boys heckled from the sidewalk. "Hit it, man! Kill it dead!"

With a hand held over his brow, Donovan squinted at the teens.

"Shouldn't those kids be in school?" Gail asked.

"It's some sort of teacher training or admin day or

something," he grumbled. "Mine are at home, too."

The boys continued their jeering, now that they'd finished their joint and apparently had nothing better to do.

Gail frowned. "Where are their parents?"

"Working, probably. Parents in this neighborhood mostly work hourly jobs. They don't show up; they don't get paid."

"Oh." She felt like a naive old biddy. "I should have guessed that."

"I only know because we get called to this neighborhood a lot," Donovan told her. He walked back to the truck, then he waved to the boys. "Farley! McDonald! Get your butts over here."

Two boys slunk over, slouching like dogs that expected to be kicked. Donovan handed them each a pair of gloves. "This is *your* neighborhood. I want that barrel full of junk"—he pointed—"in the back of that truck. And then the slide."

"Yeah, right," one of them snarled.

"Can't handle it?" Donovan put his hands on his hips. "Guess I'll have to call in the real muscle, then. Stacey, April!"

Both female firefighters looked up.

"We're doin' it, man; keep your jockstrap on." The kid called McDonald elbowed the other, and they both started toward the burn barrel. After a few minutes, their joint-smoking pals joined them, and Gail was surprised when the teens formed a line, passing armloads of trash from one to another and tossing it onto the truck bed.

She spent the morning raking up old cans and moldering items of detritus, with Marina and April at her side digging out clumps of weeds. The debris was ferried to the truck in wheelbarrows. Watching Leon heave trash and brush, Gail admired the long lean stretch of his back, the bulge of his biceps under his shirt sleeves.

By one p.m., they were all drenched in sweat, and the lot was down to bare dirt.

As Donovan drove the loaded truck away, a pizza delivery van pulled up. Leon opened the back of his SUV, transferred the pizzas to it, and pointed to two huge containers. "Cups. Plates. Water. Lemonade. Paper towels. Have at it."

Paper towels turned into black wads as they wiped hands and faces before attacking the pizzas. The teens stared hopefully at the food, scuffing their shoes in the dirt.

Leon gestured them to the back of the RAV4. "You worked; you earned it. Chow down, crew. The new equipment arrives in"—he checked his watch—"forty-two minutes."

Three younger kids who had been watching from the sidelines wandered over. The two girls and a boy stood next to the SUV door, shooting sideways glances at the pizza. Gail guessed them to be somewhere between eight and eleven years old.

Marina inserted herself between the kids and the pizza boxes. "This food's only for workers."

"What if we work?" one of the girls asked. She was a cute child, with smooth brown skin and gleaming black hair intricately braided with red beads.

"Do you promise?" Marina asked.

The kids looked at one another. The boy pushed hair out of his eyes, and the younger girl sighed dramatically as she wiped her hands on her already dirty shirt, but they both nodded at the girl with the beaded braids, who seemed to be their leader.

"Raise your right hands and repeat after me." Marina raised her own hand to demonstrate.

"I promise to work on this playground . . ."

The kids repeated the words.

". . . and take good care of it when it's finished . . . because it belongs to *our* neighborhood."

All three repeated the special emphasis on the word "our" and then, after they lowered their hands, each grabbed a slice of pizza.

Gail took her plate and sat down on the ground next to Leon. "I have blisters on my blisters, and I'm not sure I will ever stand up straight again. I'm amazed that those kids want to work."

He shrugged. "Building this is something they can point to, something they can be proud of. Everyone needs that." He lifted his slice of pizza to his lips.

I think I could love this man, a little voice said in her brain. That thought was rapidly followed by, *And then he could die.* She frowned at her traitorous conscience breaking into her pleasant fantasy.

"This pizza is the best I've ever had," she told Leon, biting into a thick piece of pepperoni.

Leon was thrilled that Gail had been so eager to join in the physical labor. A lot of women would simply have stayed in the car and cheered on the others as they worked, but Gail fit in naturally.

The project progressed swiftly after the new equipment arrived. The weather grew cloudy and the breeze picked up as everyone pitched in to assemble and place a new swing set and a climbing structure with a slide. As they worked, Leon continually scanned the bordering streets for a white Subaru until he remembered that it was Monday and Karma would be at work. There was no way the crazy woman could know where he was.

The crowning glories of the site were two solar-powered lamps on tall poles. Everyone cheered when they came on as the daylight waned. The smaller kids took the first turns on the slide, and the older ones swallowed their teen dignity to test out the swings. The whole crew high-fived to end the day, and then the adults shooed the kids home and returned to their cars.

Gail surveyed the site that now contained playground

equipment, beauty bark, and sand. "It's kind of bare. Needs a tree or two, don't you think?"

Leon grimaced. "BecauseWeShould couldn't find any company that offered free landscaping."

"I know one that might be willing to give you trees and shrubs and groundcover."

He turned to look at her. "Really?"

She twisted in her seat, reached up to brush a small clod of dirt from his hair. Her gentle fingers left an embarrassing trail of electricity in their wake. "Ever heard of a place called Langston Green?" she asked.

But the owner died. And under the new management, the business is in trouble. Insurance fraud. Failure. All the things he'd heard in the past trotted through his brain. But that was before he'd met Gail. And Elisa and Charlie.

"Well, duh," he said. "You'd be willing to donate some greenery?"

"Well, duh!" she echoed, grinning. "It's for a good cause. Of course we would. Because we should."

As he drove her back to her house, he frequently checked the rearview mirror. No white Subaru. Nor was there one in Gail's neighborhood. Her house looked tidy and untouched, as usual, although he was dismayed to see it was completely dark both inside and out. She'd left no exterior lights on in the front, nor at the side of the house where the driveway curved into the garage.

"No lights?" he asked.

She shrugged. "I didn't know we'd be getting back late. And it's a safe neighborhood."

After walking Gail to the front door, he kissed her briefly.

"I had a great day, Leon," she told him.

"Me too. Thanks for helping out and being such a good sport."

"Do you have time for dinner?"

"Not today, sorry. Gotta run." He felt a flicker of guilt as he headed to his car. But it was already seven p.m. and dark outdoors. He wanted to get back to his apartment just in case Karma showed up there again.

It was just as well that Leon didn't have time for dinner, Gail thought as she closed the door behind her. She was filthy and her refrigerator held nothing but leftovers. It had been a good, satisfying day. She'd need to consult with Elisa about donating some trees and shrubs to the project. An apple or cherry tree would be nice, as well as some species with colorful leaves in the fall. And rhodies or azaleas. That neighborhood could use some color.

Charlie wasn't home. When Gail found her cell phone, she'd probably find a text on it that said her daughter was spending the night, or at least the evening, with Jon Park. As Gail walked through the quiet living room on the way to her bedroom, she heard a faint cry outside the back door. Why did she keep hearing cats?

Peering through the glass pane at the top of the door, she saw a tiger cat sitting on the mat below. When he spotted her, his eyes widened and he meowed again.

She flicked on the exterior light, pulled the door open, and stepped outside. The cat rubbed against her ankles and repeated his pleas over and over again. He was gorgeous, a cream color with striking black stripes and swirls that formed circles over his ribs. Some sort of purebred, she'd bet. She stooped to pet him. "You need to go home, handsome. I'm sure someone is missing you."

He wouldn't stop rubbing and meowing. She could feel his ribs beneath his soft fur.

"Are you that hungry?" she asked.

He assured her that he was. She lifted him in her arms, and he bumped the top of his head against her chin, purring mightily now. Was he homeless? How could anyone abandon such a beautiful, affectionate cat?

At the corner of the house, the back gate clacked in the breeze. Odd. She'd never known the latch to come loose before. She walked to the gate, the cat nestled in her arms. The air held a faint scent of something sweet, like perfume. She sniffed again, and then noticed that the window of the house next door was open, just a crack. The neighbors must be using one of those scented oil plug-ins, or perhaps they'd spilled some perfumed household product inside.

"You didn't open this, did you?" she asked the cat as she pressed the gate back into the locked position.

She couldn't decipher anything from his purr. He head-butted her again.

"Okay, okay." She laughed and peeled a cat hair from her lower lip. "How about some canned tuna tonight? Or maybe chicken; I'll have to check. You can eat while I shower."

Chapter 16

Gail was in bed reading a book when she heard the garage door rumble up and down. The cat lay beside her on the other pillow, ears perked, staring in the direction of the noise. Wherever he'd come from, she welcomed his company and had decided not to toss him out until she was ready to turn out the light.

A minute later, Charlie called out from the living room. "Mom?"

Surprised that her daughter had come home, Gail put down the book and slid out of bed.

Charlie stood just inside the door that led to the garage. Her coat was still zipped, and her expression was troubled.

"What's up?" Gail asked.

Snatching Gail's coat from the rack beside her, Charlie held it out. "You need to see this." She flicked on the outside lights, then opened the front door and led Gail around the side of the house.

The garage door had been vandalized with spray paint. SLUT, it read, in uneven giant scarlet letters that dripped down the door like trails of blood. Gail's mouth dropped open.

"It's for me." Charlie put a hand to her throat.

"What?" Gail turned to stare at her. "Why? Or should I say who?"

Charlie groaned. "Jon has this big Korean family. Well, he was born here, but his parents and two of his older brothers emigrated from Korea."

"So?" She'd never thought of her daughter as prejudiced against immigrants.

Folding her arms across her chest, Charlie sighed. "Jon says they're really traditional. They believe that Koreans should always marry Koreans."

"You're getting married?" She put a hand on Charlie's arm. That was almost more shocking than the vandalism.

"Well, no. At least not yet." Charlie sighed again. "But Jon said he told his parents about me, and uh, it didn't go well. They want him to marry some second cousin from Korea. I was right beside him when his mother called tonight; I could hear her screeching at him even though he had the phone pressed against his ear. The conversation was all in Korean, but I'm sure Jon told her we're sleeping together. So ..." She tilted her head toward the door. "I'll get some paint and fix this tomorrow, I promise."

Gail put her arms around her daughter. "Charlene, this is not your fault."

Charlie buried her head in Gail's neck. "Oh God, what am I going to do? I think I love Jon, and his family hates me. And they don't even know me!"

"I'm sure that's the problem," Gail murmured into her daughter's blond hair. "When they do know you, they'll love you."

"Uh-huh." Charlie didn't sound so sure, and when she raised her head, her cheeks were streaked with tears.

"Don't worry about this. We'll fix it together." Gail rested her forehead against her daughter's. "Let's go back into the house and have a glass of wine."

They sat at the kitchen table and Gail poured each of them a glass of sauvignon blanc. "I'm glad you're home tonight, Charlie. I want to tell you about my day."

"*Your* day?" Her daughter lifted her wine glass, then abruptly yelped, jerking her hand and sloshing a splash of wine onto the table. "What the heck?" Scooting back her chair, she peered under the table.

Then Gail felt the tiger cat rub against her bare ankles. "Oh," she murmured, reaching down to pet him. "I'd forgotten he was here."

Charlie scowled at her. "Did Leon give you this cat?"

Gail frowned back. "Why would you assume that?"

Her daughter shrugged. "You two have been together a lot, and you're doing all kinds of crazy things, like the rafting and art projects and snorkeling in the pool, and I just thought . . ." She let the sentence drift off.

Gail lifted the cat into her lap. "For your information, this cat adopted *me*. And he was hungry." She stroked the cat, who slit his green eyes and lifted his chin for a scratch. "Why do you say the other things I've been doing are crazy?"

Charlie studied her wine glass, ran her thumb down through the condensation that was forming on the outside. "Well, crazy might be too strong a word. It's just"—she glanced at the family photo on the wall—"so much has changed since Dad died."

"Of course it has," Gail murmured.

"*I* miss him every day," Charlie said. "If Dad were still here, he'd talk to Jon's parents."

Guilt wafted like a gust of warm air through the kitchen, and Gail experienced an odd desire to purse her lips and blow it away. Did Charlie really expect her to keep her life exactly the same, as a memorial to Terry? Gail swallowed, wet her lips, and chose her words carefully.

"I know you're upset about the garage door, Charlene. I understand that. And yes, I miss your father, too. I'm still grieving over losing Terry and the wonderful life we had together for so long."

"*Life is for the living*," said Leon's voice in her head. Gail took a sip of wine before continuing. "But Terry is gone, and we all have to solve our own problems now. I'm not a fossil. And this house is not a museum."

Charlie's blue eyes remained accusatory, even as they filled with tears. Gail's heart ached. Charlie had always been a soft-hearted drama queen, while Elisa had always been a fierce child who hid her feelings. Both her girls had experienced loss several times over: Charlie with the deaths of Mark and Terry, Elisa with the desertion of her mother and then with her father's death. But they were in their thirties now, for heaven's sake. Elisa had far more problems to deal with at the nursery, but she seemed to be coping, while Charlie was shredding like wet tissue paper because of an epithet spray-painted on a garage door.

Had she been so fixated on her own grief that she'd ignored her daughter's sorrow? Was she being selfish?

The cat butted his head against her chin again, and she stroked him as her gaze shifted to the family portrait on the wall. *Oh, Terry, how could you go, too, just like the others? Where's my support system?* If only Leon was sitting beside her; she could really use his strength right now. Or Jeannie. But Jeannie had Gary. Leon was busy living his own life, his days full of friends and meaningful work and adventure. He'd clearly been in a hurry to get somewhere after he'd dropped her off this evening.

Buck up, Gail told herself, shifting her gaze back to her daughter. Charlie was missing Terry. What would her husband have done right now? She moved her hand from the cat's striped head to Charlie's shoulder.

"I'll talk to Jon's parents," she volunteered.

Charlie's eyes rounded with alarm. "Oh God, no, Mom! *Please* stay out of it," she begged, sounding more like a teenager than an independent young woman. Then she stood up. "I don't want to think about it any longer. I'm going to bed."

At least Charlie didn't flounce from the room like she had as a seventeen-year-old. For a long stretch, Gail sat in her chair, staring mournfully at all the family photos on the wall, the frozen mementos of an earlier happy life.

Chapter 17

Leon was relieved when he didn't spot Karma's car in the parking lot of his apartment complex. He held his breath as he unlocked the door of his apartment, but there was no sign of her inside, either. Had she finally given up on pursuing him?

He'd only slipped one arm out of his jacket when his cell phone chimed. There was his answer: Karma was calling. Don't engage, he told himself. But no sooner than the ringtone had stopped, it started again. If he didn't answer, he was afraid she would stop by in person. He picked up the phone.

"Karma, please stop calling," he said. "How many times do I have to tell you I'm not interested?"

"Hi, babe! I drove by that corner lot on my way home, and wow! You guys really transformed it."

Leon frowned at the phone. How did Karma know where he'd been today? "What are you talking about?"

"I google you all the time, you know. I think it's wonderful that you volunteer for BecauseWeShould."

Shit! His name was on the list of volunteers on that site. And so was the list of their projects. Damn social media.

"I'm hurt that you didn't ask me to help. I would have loved to do that."

He was grateful that she hadn't driven by while the whole crew was there. "I'm sure you had to work, and we didn't need any more help."

"Amazon gives us days off for volunteer work."

"Good for them," he said. "Goodbye, Karma." He pulled

the phone away from his ear and stretched a finger for the "End" button.

"Wait! You'll want to hear this!"

Against his better judgment, he lifted the phone again.

"I got Seahawks tickets for next Sunday for both of us!"

He sighed. "Take a friend. I'm not interested. Stop calling me, stop texting me, stop coming by. If I ever find you've broken into my apartment again, I'll have you charged with breaking and entering or burglary."

"I didn't steal anything. I'll bet you love to sleep with your head on that pillowcase with my thong right next to you."

"I threw them both away. And why did you have to destroy my painting?"

There was a brief pause, then she said, "It didn't belong there."

Did she know it had come from Gail? It hadn't been signed, had it?

"I can find you a much better painting that that," she offered. "One that goes with your style. As a matter of fact, why don't we redecorate your whole apartment? I'm great at interior design, and it would be fun. I could come over right now and we could get started."

"Don't. I won't let you in. I'm going to bed."

"Poor tired baby! Okay, rain check on the decoration project, but I can't wait; we always have such good times together. I'm sending you a little reminder of our good times right now."

His cell chimed in his ear and he pulled the phone away to look at the screen. She'd sent him a photo of herself in what was clearly his bed, and she'd put a printed photo of his face next to her on the pillow. In the picture, he wore the white cap of his dress uniform. He recognized it as a crop from his photo on the fire station website. Karma's accompanying text message read *See you soon!*

Crap! She'd obviously copied that photo from the web, printed it, and taken a selfie with it on the night he'd found her in his apartment. A spark of alarm flamed in his chest. Karma could easily decide to post that on Facebook or send that all over the place.

Instead of pressing "End," he turned the cell phone off.

Chapter 18

Leon said BecauseWeShould appreciated the azaleas and apple trees that Langston Green donated for the new playground, but he invited only Donovan Kelly to help him plant them with Gail. The three of them did it on a Monday morning, and Gail thought Leon seemed in a hurry to get the task over with. This planting project had none of the flavor of a group endeavor like the initial project had, and she was disappointed not to see the rest of the BecauseWeShould crowd again. After he drove her home, she'd offered Leon lunch at her house.

"Nothing fancy," she told him. "Just tomato soup and toasted cheese sandwiches. But you seem to be in a rush. Do you need to be somewhere this afternoon?"

"Nowhere special. Having lunch with you would be great."

After fifteen minutes of nuking the soup and grilling the sandwiches, she called him in from the living room. Pulling himself away from the front window he'd been staring out of, he sat down at the kitchen table, visibly relaxing his shoulders. Gesturing toward his soup bowl and sandwich plate, he smiled at her. "This is nice, Gail. Your house is always so welcoming, so homey."

"I'd love to see your place," she told him.

"No, you wouldn't." He took a bite of his sandwich and chewed for a few seconds before continuing, "It's only a basic two-bedroom apartment. I don't have pillows on the couch or art on the walls like you do." Then, as if he'd only just remembered, he added, "Except for your beautiful painting, of course. But otherwise, it's devoid of any personality. Basically, I only sleep there. I guess I've never really tried to make it feel like home."

"I could help you give it some personality," she suggested. "Help you decorate it?"

His expression froze at those words, his jaw tightening and his eyes widening in something like alarm. Instead of putting his soup spoon to his lips, he put it back into his bowl.

What was *that* about?

"Only if you want help," she hastily added. "I didn't mean to imply . . ." She didn't know how to finish that sentence.

Leon's stricken look evaporated as if it had never been there. He nodded politely and picked up his spoon again. "I'll have you over sometime soon."

Gail focused on cutting her cheese sandwich into halves. Why didn't he want her to see where he lived? Was Leon living with another woman? If that were true, surely Charlie would have wormed that information out of Jon by now. Maybe she was pushing herself on him, assuming he would welcome her to every aspect of his life? Squelching her bruised feelings, she murmured, "Leon, I don't expect to be the only woman you're seeing—"

"No, that's not it at all, Gail." After wiping his hand on his napkin, he reached across the table and squeezed her fingers. "I do want you to come over, but only after I have a chance to fix up the place a little. Trust me, you don't want to see it now." He picked up his sandwich again.

She thought they'd been getting along so well, and she'd looked forward to every opportunity to be with Leon. But today he'd acted rushed and eager to leave, citing the prediction of rain for the afternoon even while the sky was perfectly clear. She didn't have a clue what was going on, and she didn't really know how to act. Obviously, Leon Maxwell didn't want her to be part of his everyday world.

Forcing a note of cheer into her voice, she told him, "I have chocolate chip cookies for dessert."

After Leon left, Gail pulled on a jacket to go for a stroll around the neighborhood. The sun would not set until after six p.m. today, but now, at just a few minutes before three, the sky was already growing dark with clouds, and she wanted to walk off some of her uneasiness. Whenever she and Terry had a disagreement or needed to make some major decision, they had gone for long walks while they talked. Walking always helped. They might start off bitterly divided on some topic, but after a few blocks they'd be admiring a neighbor's daffodils or laughing at the way a Douglas squirrel angrily scolded a dog peeing on the base of the squirrel's tree.

As she paced along the sidewalk, she reviewed her morning with Leon. He'd seemed distracted, hadn't he? Or reluctant to spend more time with her, somehow? Was she too boring? Not vivacious enough? Was he impatient to meet up with the mysterious Karma who called him?

God, she missed Terry, their easy roles, their comfortable life together. They'd often strolled these streets hand in hand, especially in the warmer months. She missed his arms around her, his lips on hers, their relaxed conversation about the minutiae of their lives.

"Oh, sweetheart, you left such a hole in my world," she murmured softly to herself, fingering the locket he'd given her. "Marrying you was supposed to be my last big decision. I don't know how to do this solo act again."

The cold wind was picking up, matching her mood, and she jammed her hands into her pockets and increased her pace. A block down from her house, she spotted the tiger cat sitting on the front porch of a house that sported a new FOR SALE sign. The cat sat with his back to the street, swishing his ringed tail and staring at the front door as if willing it to open.

She walked up the sidewalk to the front steps. "Hey, bud."

The cat turned his green eyes in her direction and mewed a soft note. She stroked his head, and he began to purr but rubbed his length against the front door instead of against her legs. No lights were visible in the house, but she rang the doorbell anyway. She heard the chime echo hollowly inside.

There was no answer. The cat rose up onto his hind feet, placing his front feet high up on the door and sinking his claws into the screen as he meowed.

After he dropped back onto all fours, she pulled open the screen door and knocked on the wood-paneled door inside. "Hello?"

The neighbor's front porch light snapped on, and an elderly woman wearing a blue cardigan stuck her head out. "There's nobody home over there. Call the Realtor's number on the sign, dear."

"I'm not looking for a house," Gail explained. She pointed toward the tiger cat. "I'm wondering about this cat. I'm Gail Langston. I live down the street, and this cat has visited me several times, but it looks as if he wants to get inside this house. Does he belong here?"

The woman stepped outside, letting the door close behind her, and focused on the cat. "Oh, dear. That's Orion. He's Tom Simpson's cat."

"Is Mr. Simpson on vacation?"

"Mmmm." The woman pressed her lips together and wrung her hands. She studied the cat for a long moment before lifting her eyes to Gail. "Tom died about two weeks ago. He was ninety-two."

"I'm so sorry," Gail murmured. "Who's taking care of Orion?"

"Tom didn't have any family here. The Realtor told me a nephew in Oregon decided to put the house up for sale." The woman pulled her cardigan closed and wrapped her arms around her chest. "I guess Orion got left behind. You should probably take him to the pound." Then she scanned the darkening sky. "It's going to rain soon, isn't it? I'd better be getting back inside." The door closed behind her.

The first raindrops plopped across Gail's shoulders. The cat gazed up at her and mewed again. He rubbed against her calves, then again faced the door and stretched his front paws up as high as he could, staring at the wooden panels and meowing insistently.

Orion had been looking for a dead man for two weeks.

Tears blurred Gail's vision. She picked up the cat, buried her face in his warm fur. "I know, sweetie. Believe me, I know."

Chapter 19

After she and Jeannie had painted and bedazzled them with sequins and glitter, Gail's little sculptures of fairies and dragonflies and butterflies looked fantastic on their sticks. They instantly made her shop more festive, and after selling a few mixed in with flowers for personalized bouquets, word began to spread, and some customers came in to buy them as standalone gifts. Inspired, Gail and Jeannie were transforming some of their designs into Christmas ornaments for the upcoming season.

Life seemed to be looking up for Elisa and Langston Green, too. Harvest Fest had been an unexpected drama but ended mostly happily with the long-awaited exposure of the vandal who had been terrorizing the nursery. It looked as if that side of the family business would get back on track now, and although she was proud of her daughter, Gail chafed a bit at how well Elisa was managing the nursery without her mother's help. The survival of Gail's Seattle florist shop was still up in the air, but for now, she decided to embrace the challenges of scuba class and creating art and trying to make a richer life for herself.

The clay tab on the back of the library lady broke off the first time Gail pushed it onto the lip of a pot, but she and Jeannie had improved on the original design with metal tabs embedded in the clay before firing, and they were having fun creating elves and pixies and humans of all persuasions and colors in seated positions, in costumes or with props that indicated their hobbies or professions.

So far, they had mothers and fathers with babes in arms, children holding puppies and kittens, readers with books in their laps, scientists with test tubes in hand, artists, and sculptors. They were working on police officers and soldiers, which they'd at first found problematic because neither of them wanted to add a gun to the ornament. Finally, they decided to position them with arms crossed. Then they received a few requests for programmers and finally came up with geeky sculptures of a man and woman, seated and holding laptops.

Jeannie's constant Facebook postings of their creations brought a modest wave of new customers into Gail's shop. After a few weeks, it still wasn't enough business to make a big profit, but for a change, Gail's Flowers was a store with a growing clientele.

Jeannie suggested they might sell their creations via the internet. They'd discussed that over lunch one day, initially excited about the idea. Then, as the need for mass production occurred to both of them, they decided to keep the project simple, fun, and local. The whole idea was to add a personal touch, and mass-produced items were as far from personal as anyone could get.

Although they still created the sculptures at Jeannie's house, Gail worked on painting and adding the final touches in the back of her shop. She was working on a new idea, a parrot perching on the pot or vase edge and looking back over its shoulder. She was trying to decide exactly which colors to paint its feathers when her shop bell rang.

The customer was a woman around Charlie's age, with curly black hair. She had one of Gail's reader sculptures in hand, and she waved it in the air. "You make these, right?"

"Most of them," Gail admitted, nodding at the shelf of her creations. "Some are made by a friend. It's sort of a hobby, I guess you'd say."

"They're wonderful. I'm a reporter for *Seattle Weekly*, and I'd like to do a story on you."

"Really?"

"Really. Can we talk now?"

Gail looked through the windows toward the street. No customers in sight. "Yes, I guess so. Do you want to come on into the back room?"

The woman pulled out her cell phone. "Can I take a few photos out here first?" She pressed a thumb against the device and the little flash went off, startling Gail.

"Can I at least comb my hair?"

"No need. You look great." She plucked a few of the stick sculptures from the vase on the counter and held them out to Gail. "How about a pose with these?"

As soon as Gail had them in hand, the woman snapped another picture. Yeesh. This was all happening way too fast. "What did you say your name was?"

"Sierra Weisel, from *Seattle Weekly*."

"Come on back, Sierra." Gail gestured her around the counter. "As you can see, we're not exactly swamped with business right now."

"This article might change that," Sara said brightly.

We'll see, Gail thought, not daring to hope for too much. She was learning that was the key to happiness: not to expect too much.

That seemed to be the key to her relationship with Leon, too. He was working extra shifts, but when he was off, he called her. With him, Gail was rediscovering her love of nature. On clear days, they went hiking in the Cascade foothills. The forests and streams of the lowlands were beautiful all year round, while the peaks were often frosted with snow now that the calendar was sliding toward winter. The awkwardness between her and Leon had vanished, or maybe she'd only imagined it. She'd just been too forward, trying to insert herself into his life. Despite what he had told her on their night out at The Bayou, Leon Maxwell was apparently a very private man.

Scuba lessons remained her secret, shared only with Jeannie. The first time the scuba students put their regulators into their mouths and sank beneath the surface of the swimming pool, Gail fell in love with scuba diving. She no longer had to hold her breath, waiting for the next opportunity to lift her head and inhale. She could breathe underwater. That new ability made even the mundane swimming pool seem like a totally new environment. No wonder Leon and his friends talked about their diving experiences with rapture in their voices.

The emergency drills in the pool were frightening, though. Removing her mask reduced the surroundings to an eye-stinging blur; she had to fight down hysteria each time she was forced to do it. She never succeeded in putting her mask back on without pulling hair between the mask and her face. Forcing the water out of the mask by exhaling air into it through her nose seemed to take forever, and then she still had to pull strands of hair from under the mask to prevent a constant dribble of water inside.

Out-of-air drills were even worse. Each one seemed like an opportunity for disaster, even in the pool. She hated to take the regulator out of her own mouth and buddy-breathe, sharing air with another diver. It was nerve-racking to drop her weights and try to ascend slowly, exhaling all the way to the surface to prevent rupturing a lung or getting the bends. How could any diver manage to do it from a hundred feet down?

But after learning about how a diver could kill herself by streaking to the surface, she understood the need to practice handling emergencies underwater. At least her logical mind did. Her more primal instincts fought the logic every time, leaving her feeling panicked before each drill.

There were so many ways to die underwater.

Had Keith and Mark and Terry ever thought about dying?

Leon rushed into fires and dashed into the midst of horrific accidents and illnesses that could easily be deadly, but he never seemed to think about how his own life might end, although he'd shared a few stories of patients who hadn't lived to reach the emergency room. *"Life is for the living."* His days were ruled by that creed.

In the classroom, there were lectures on the dangers of sharks and stonefish and sea urchins, downdrafts and upswells and fierce currents. She simply wanted to float among the fish and enjoy the view—couldn't she just do that? She was proud that she had the floating thing down, the star of the class. Neutral buoyancy, they called it. With the right amount of air in her buoyancy vest, her arms folded across her chest and her feet still, she could hover in place like a hummingbird.

"You're a natural," the instructor, Richard, told her in the third week of lessons. "But I'm sure you understand that the open ocean is a little more challenging than the pool."

Chapter 20

Orion, like the constellation he was named after, was a creature of the night. If the moon was full, he stayed out until dawn, and once he gifted her with a dead mouse, which she didn't especially appreciate. When the weather was grim, the cat sometimes deigned to stay inside after dark, curled up in Gail's bedroom on the pillow that used to be Terry's. Orion had made it clear that Gail was to keep the curtains open to the backyard so he could keep watch, and he slept in the patch of starry light that filtered in. She liked waking up to find the cat next to her, to be able to stroke his soft fur and hear his reassuring purr after a haunting dream.

But the cat sometimes snored, and at other times he whined and mewled as he twitched, either hunting or being hunted in his dreams. One night he abruptly leaped to his feet, and Gail woke to find him hissing and growling, his back hunched as he stared at the backyard through the parted curtains.

She sat up. "What?"

He growled, still focused on the window. She started to put out a hand, but then was afraid to touch him and spook him further. "It's okay, bud," she told him. "There's nothing out there."

At least she hoped that was true. Sliding out of bed, she shuffled to the window and peered out. The bare limbs of the trees were moving in a light breeze and clouds scudded across the sky, but she saw no movement, nothing out of place.

"Was it a raccoon?" she asked the cat.

Orion continued to growl as he jumped from the bed and padded down the hall to the back door. Gail followed him, wondering whether she should arm herself with a knife or frying pan or something, wishing Charlie were home with her.

A clack sounded outside. A raccoon on the trash can? The cat scratched at the door. She didn't want Orion to tangle with a wild animal.

"You stay in the background," she warned Orion. "I'll take care of the raccoon." Arming herself with a broom from the closet, she opened the back door and peered out. The cat escaped through the opening, trotting toward the back gate, which was swinging, unlatched, in the wind. He sat down close by and watched the gate clack against the fence post.

"Was there a raccoon?" she asked him, peering down the side of the house toward the garage door. No masked bandits. And no graffiti, thank heavens. She pushed the gate closed and latched it firmly. Near the back door, the garbage can appeared to be intact, untouched. "If there was a raccoon, you scared him off, Orion."

Bending, she petted the cat's head. "Or maybe it was just the wind?" He butted his striped head against her leg and purred. "I'm freezing. Aren't you?"

When Gail hustled back to the door, the cat insisted on staying outside. She stroked his head. "Oh, sweetie, you won't find him, no matter how often you go back to your old house."

Orion still refused to come in. "Be that way," she said. "But don't come scratching and yowling around and waking me up before daylight, okay?"

She locked the door behind her, and as she slipped back into her bed, she heard a car drive down the street. Then another car engine and the whap of a rolled-up newspaper hitting her front sidewalk. Just normal night sounds.

Two days later, as she was raking leaves, she was startled

to find a dead rat beneath her bedroom window. When she bent to examine it, she had to stifle a scream. The rat had been neatly decapitated. Its body faced downward, resting on its paws, but its head faced upward, its beady eyes staring skyward from between its two front paws. Holding her breath against the foul smell, she tied the little corpse up in a plastic bag and put it into the trash.

"You're not becoming a serious predator, are you?" she asked the cat. "Is that what you do at night, look for things to kill?"

Orion gave her a squinty look of feline disdain and then went back to washing his face with a curled paw.

"Just don't do it again, okay? That rat almost gave me a heart attack."

Chapter 21

Leon dreaded the mail delivery each day. First, Karma had left him a package at his front door, a paper-wrapped painting of a couple hand in hand, silhouetted against a sunset. The painting was actually quite attractive, but he sent it back. Next, she sent him tickets to a play, which he also promptly returned, then a copy of the Kama Sutra, which he threw away. Twice, she showed up at the fire station during his shifts, and he refused to come out of his sleeping quarters. His colleagues treated the situation like it was a joke.

It was humiliating. She hadn't broken into his apartment again, thank heavens, but she continued to knock on his door and leave embarrassing notes and photos on the windshield of his SUV. The woman was relentless. Just this morning he'd found an invitation to Thanksgiving dinner at her house next week. He declined via text, and again asked her to stop communicating with him at all.

When Gail told him about the slur sprayed on her garage door, Leon's first thought had been Karma. But Gail's daughter Charlie seemed to think that Jon Park's relatives were responsible, and Jon also thought that might be a possibility, although he said his brothers had vehemently denied it.

Karma had also instantly leaped to mind when Gail told him about the decapitated rat. But Gail had recently adopted a cat, and she blamed the corpse on his nocturnal hunts. As far as Leon knew, Karma did not have Gail's address or phone number, and he was determined to keep it that way.

He and Jon were taking inventory of the supplies in the aid truck at the station when Stacey knocked on the open door. "Maxwell, there's a visitor at the front desk for you."

He hesitated.

Stacey put her hands on her hips. "It's not Karma."

Shoving his clipboard into Jon's hands, Leon stepped down from the truck and made his way from the garage to the front of the station. The visitor was a chubby woman with a pleasant freckled face and graying red hair. He didn't recognize her. But as an EMT, he frequently crossed paths with all sorts of people, and occasionally they stopped by the station to thank him or ask a question.

"Leo Maxwell, right?" the woman chirped.

"It's Leon, actually."

"Really? Since when?"

What? "I'm sorry, I don't remember your name."

The woman waved a plump hand in the air. "Well, naturally you wouldn't, seeing as how we've never met. I'm Twyla Woodstone, Karma's sister. I can't believe I'm finally meeting you! You are just as handsome as your photos. We keep asking Karma to bring you over for Sunday dinner."

Leon had no idea how to respond to that. But he didn't need to, as Twyla twittered on. "Karma is always showing off your picture and telling us about all the heroic deeds you do with the fire department. But"—she lowered her voice and put her hand on his forearm—"I don't understand why you insist on keeping your engagement a secret. You're not married, are you? Karma can be so gullible sometimes; I worry about her."

An ache began behind Leon's left eyebrow. "Twyla, Karma and I are not engaged." He gently detached the woman's hand from his arm. "We're not even dating. In fact, Karma and I *never* dated."

She stared at him, open-mouthed. He noticed her cherry-red lipstick was a tiny bit smeared. "But I've seen the photos," she said. "Your apartment, the fire station, your friends at The Bayou . . . And those bouquets you send her— all those red roses!"

Sweet Jesus, it was worse than he thought. "Twyla, your sister follows me around. Our relationship exists only in her imagination. Please ask Karma to leave me alone."

The woman's forehead creased. "Oh, no. No, no, no! You just want to play the field, don't you? Karma will be crushed; she adores you. She's planning on spending her life with you. But you, you're planning to break her heart, aren't you?"

He folded his arms across his chest. "Again, Twyla, Karma and I do not currently have, nor have we *ever* had, a romantic relationship. Please tell her to leave me alone."

She made a scoffing noise. "I can't believe this! She says only the nicest things about you."

The ache behind Leon's eyebrow spread. Now his whole head was throbbing.

The lieutenant appeared at the front desk behind them with a stack of reports in his hand. Leon was painfully aware of his boss's presence.

Twyla glared at Leon for a long moment, her facial expression morphing into a squinty-eyed scowl. Raising her voice, she snarled, "I think you're scum!"

He held up both hands. "Lady, look—"

She poked a scarlet-nailed finger into his chest. "How could you?"

Grabbing her arm, he pulled her through the station doors into the parking lot. "Look, Miss Woodstone—"

She jerked her arm from his grasp. "Mrs."

He folded his arms across his chest again. "Mrs. Woodstone, we have a misunderstanding here. I never—"

"That's so cruel. Karma's already planning the wedding." She rubbed her arms as if he'd bruised it.

"I don't know what Karma has told you, but—"

She jabbed him again with a finger. "She told the whole family how much she loved you, that's what!"

"I'm sorry about that, but you have to understand that the attraction was never mutual. We were only together once." *And you have no idea how much I regret that,* he added in his head.

The woman rolled her eyes. "Oh, please. Don't lie to me. Karma's told us about all the times she's been with you. About how you were going to buy a house together, about the two kids you both wanted."

Leon felt the muscles tighten between his shoulder blades. "Your sister is delusional. She may even need psychiatric help. I never made any promises to Karma."

Twyla Woodstone tilted her head. "Then why did you give her an engagement ring?"

"I didn't. She's wearing a ring?" Did he truly deserve this, just for a one-night stand? Did any man? He pressed a hand against his throbbing temple. "I—"

Abruptly, the woman slapped him. "Scum!" she screeched. "You don't deserve her, but she loves you. I came here to personally invite you for Thanksgiving dinner, but now I'll lock the door if I see you coming."

Turning on her heel, the woman bobbled angrily toward a car parked in the visitor's slot and then, squealing the tires, she peeled out of the lot.

Leon stood in the cold darkness for a minute, rubbing his stinging cheek. When he walked back inside, the lieutenant was still at the front desk, and now he was glaring at him. "Maxwell," he growled. "What the hell? You're on duty. Good thing it's dark outside and the public didn't witness any of that. You're the most experienced guy here; you should know the rules of conduct."

"This is not—"

The lieutenant cut him off with a slash of his hand through the air. "Get your love life in order."

The radio blared. Leon had never been so grateful to hear the call for EMTs and the aid truck.

Chapter 22

At its beginning, Gail's first open-water dive was disappointing. From the beach, she plowed through eelgrass and silt kicked up by the other students ahead of her in the cold, murky water of Puget Sound. Then, when they reached deeper water, she knelt on the bottom with the others to do the dreaded drills. During the mask removal and replacement, Gail's blood pressure shot up, but she made her way through the motions, relieved when the air she exhaled into her mask finally allowed her to see again.

Then Richard swam to her, drawing his hand horizontally across his throat—out of air, out of air! She sucked in a breath, exchanged her regulator for her spare, and then handed him her primary. Relief flooded her chest when he made the okay sign with his fingers to show she'd passed the test.

After the drills, the group swam along the shoreline beneath a dock, where Gail discovered to her amazement that underwater, barnacles were truly beautiful creatures. Those ugly gray shells hid delicate white, feathery fronds that the shellfish gracefully waved to filter plankton from the water. An orange sun star crawled across the sandy bottom, and half a dozen purple starfish clung to a piling among tubeworms, whose ugly brown casings enclosed more feathery filter feeders. If any of these creatures had a head, she didn't recognize it. It was a whole different world down here. She hung in the water, admiring the sea life, careful not to touch anything.

By the time Richard gave the class the turn-around sign, Gail was freezing from the frigid Puget Sound water. As they finned their way back to the beach, two silver fish flitted past in front of her, and she spied a slender green pipefish head down, hiding among the eelgrass. It seemed like an all-too-brief visit to another planet.

"Congratulations," Richard said to the seven of them who had persisted and finished the course. "You are now certified divers."

Gail invited Leon, Jon, and Elisa's investigator-turned-lover, Jake, for Thanksgiving, but she didn't want to play the grand hostess and cook a huge meal as she had for the last twenty years. She settled for baking the turkey and assigned everyone else a dish to bring. Charlie gave her a disappointed look but agreed that she and Jon would bring the pies for dessert. Elisa and Jake volunteered for potatoes and bread, and Leon seemed happy to bring a vegetable dish.

Gail didn't want him to think she was a hausfrau who did nothing except cook and clean. She no longer wanted him to assume anything about her.

It was nice to have the whole family together, and this year the group had expanded even further, with the three new men and even children this time. Seated between Elisa and Charlie were Elisa's newly discovered relatives from Guatemala, Timo Martinez and his baby sister, Rosa. Gail was glad that she had no empty chairs, nothing except her memories to remind her of Terry's absence.

They went around the table, saying why they were thankful on the holiday. When it was Jon's turn, he—of course—looked at Charlie and said he was thankful for meeting her. And then he turned to Gail. "And I'm thankful to you, Gail, for sending that beautiful arrangement to my mother."

Charlie twisted in her seat to look at Jon with

astonishment. "What?" Then she swiveled toward Gail. "Oh, Mom, you didn't!"

Jon put a calming hand on the back of Charlie's neck as he continued to hold Gail's gaze. "The way you showed how Charlie and I and our families could fit together to make a beautiful bouquet was incredible. My mother may not understand English well, but it seems she understands the language of flowers."

Charlie's expression wavered.

"You were a pink Gerbera daisy," Jon told her. "And I was a very handsome exotic green orchid. Then my mom was an Oriental lily and my dad and brothers were Lotus pods, and there were two other white daisies—"

"For me and Elisa," Gail chimed in.

"And there were butterflies on sticks and a pharmacist sitting on the edge of the vase. It was incredible."

Charlie turned to Gail, her cheeks aflame. "How'd you know Jon's father was a pharmacist?"

Gail tilted her head toward Leon.

Leon chuckled. "There are few secrets in a fire station. Jon's mother still does his laundry, by the way."

Jon scowled at his partner. "She does not! At least not all the time." He turned back to Gail. "Anyhow, that bouquet turned the tide," he concluded.

Dipping her chin, Charlie softly said, "Thanks, Mom."

When everyone had dessert and coffee on the table, Gail excused herself to go to her bedroom. Slipping out of her slacks and sweater, she donned her new wetsuit and pulled her scuba mask on top of her forehead. Orion studied her from his position on her bed, flicking his tail. "No judging," she warned him.

The tiger cat went back to licking a paw as if such a thought would never cross his mind. Picking up her new certification card from the dresser, Gail screwed up her courage and strode into the dining room.

"Tah-dah!" she exclaimed, throwing out her hands.

They all gaped at her for a long moment. Then Charlie said, "Oh God, Mom, what have you done?"

Elisa was confused. "What's going on?"

"I'm a certified scuba diver now," Gail explained. "I passed the test yesterday."

"Whoa!" Elisa said. "Unexpected."

Gail glanced at Leon. He grinned and shouted, "Yahoo!" as he extended a hand toward her.

She grasped his fingers. "Maybe we could go diving together in the San Juans sometime next summer." Did that sound pushy? She quickly added, "We could invite Stacey and Donovan and April and Conrad."

Leon reeled her into his lap. "You're coming with us to Roatan!"

"Oh, no. I didn't mean to horn in on your adventure; I just thought we could dive together sometime in the future. It's too late to get a plane ticket for Christmas. I'm sure everything's all booked up by now. You have your reservations. And I'm not a real diver yet."

Pulling out his cell phone, Leon began to text with his thumbs. "I have space in my bungalow. And"—he pressed his thumb on the phone, then held it up for her to view the screen—"I just bought you a plane ticket."

Gail checked her daughters' expressions across the table. Elisa was grinning as she entwined her fingers with Jake's. Charlie appeared to be stunned. Gail turned back to Leon. "Oh, I didn't intend for you to—"

"You're going to love it," he interrupted, hugging her tighter. "Our bungalow is out over the water; you can see stingrays and fish from the balcony."

Our bungalow. He did look genuinely happy. Her heart lifted.

Leon pulled the certification card out of her hand and waved it in the air. "This proves you're a real diver. Yes! Christmas in the Caribbean with a hot woman!" He pressed his lips to the card and then turned his head and pulled her down for a kiss.

For more than twenty years, Gail had trusted Terry Langston with her feelings. Could she trust Leon? They hadn't even made love yet. But at this moment, his beaming expression told her she should take the risk.

Christmas would not be a lonely affair with an empty place for Terry. There would be tropical flowers and warm water and new adventures, and her holidays would be spent with friends.

When Elisa and Timo and Rosa started clapping. Gail leaned close to Leon's ear. "Stay with me tonight?"

Leon's eyes lit up. His breath warmed her cheek as he whispered back, "I thought you'd never ask."

Before she slipped between the sheets later that evening, Gail finally found the courage to take off her wedding ring. She placed it in her jewelry box next to the antique locket. And then she turned to the gorgeous, virile man in her bed.

Gently tracing the curve of his jaw with her finger, Gail welcomed him with a tender kiss. "I'm grateful that you're here, Leon. Happy Thanksgiving."

Rising onto one elbow, he pressed her back onto her pillow. "I'm grateful that I met you, Gail Grace Langston. This is the happiest Thanksgiving ever."

I've finally learned how to do it. I'm living for today. I'm having fun, Jeannie.

Chapter 23

It was a bit of a shock to see Leon's head on Terry's pillow the next morning. His eyes were open and he was watching her. Above his head, Orion perched on the bookcase headboard and studied the man below with his intense green eyes. Leon smiled and pulled Gail close. "Still grateful?"

"Am I going to have to thank you every time we make love?"

He laughed. "You mean you're already taking me for granted?"

"Time will tell." She ran a hand over the smooth hard muscles of Leon's chest and stomach, so different from Terry's furrier, softer form. Then she rolled over on top of him. "I'm grateful that we have the house to ourselves."

"We are not exactly alone." Chuckling, Leon reached up and stroked the cat's head.

"Close your eyes, Orion." Gail pressed her lips to Leon's.

Later, in the kitchen, Leon made coffee, and then, as she relaxed at the kitchen table, he set about making breakfast. "You don't have to do that—" she began.

He pulled his head out of the refrigerator to look at her. "I love to cook."

"Really?" She found it difficult to imagine him doing something so domestic.

"Why do you sound so surprised?"

"You told me you're never in your apartment." She regretted those words the second they escaped her mouth.

Maybe Leon cooked in other women's apartments.

He shrugged. "It's no fun to cook for myself." After pulling out a carton of eggs, he rummaged through the refrigerator drawers and extracted a variety of leftover vegetables, cheese, and turkey. Finding her skillet in the drawer beneath the stove and some spices on the shelf, he worked on producing an imaginative omelet.

As she watched him mince peppers and onions, she said, "I've been thinking about that playground project. Based on the size of that lot, I wondered whether the neighborhood might welcome a pea patch project—you know, a place to plant flowers and vegetables and such. Langston Green could supply some seeds and starts and lend a rototiller to prepare an area."

"Gail, that's a wonderful idea. Most of those folks live in apartments and have no garden space of their own. I'll bring it up with BecauseWeShould. There are a lot of other abandoned lots on our list, too."

The cat wound around their ankles as they ate breakfast together, and at one point, Orion leaped into Leon's lap without an invitation.

"Sorry," Gail apologized. "His previous owner was a man who lived down the street. He died."

"I like cats." Leon stroked Orion from head to tail, and the cat rubbed his head against Leon's chest. "I'm sorry for your loss, buddy. But I'm not sharing my omelet." He gently placed the cat back on the ground.

They talked about small details of their everyday lives. "Are you a sports fan?" she asked with some trepidation. "Do you watch games on TV?"

"Not really," he admitted. "The occasional Super Bowl party with friends, but I don't care who wins. I always root for the underdog." Then his expression grew alarmed. "Are you a big sports fan? I mean, I could get into it if—"

She laughed. "Relax. I never even know whether it's

basketball or football season. Or baseball, I forgot that. Oh, and I guess there's hockey and soccer now, too. Did I leave anything out?"

"Rugby?"

"Do we have a rugby team in Washington state?"

Chuckling, he told her, "Truth be told, I spend more time reading than watching television."

She took another bite of omelet. "I'm addicted to mysteries."

He pointed to himself. "Sci-fi. And the occasional biography." When she didn't immediately respond, he raised one silvered eyebrow. "Did you honestly think I spent all my time pulling people out of burning buildings and bungee jumping? I don't have enough energy for nonstop action."

"Oh, thank God." She smiled at him. "I was so afraid you were constantly looking for thrills."

"Not constantly," he said. "Sometimes I have to stop and do mundane things. Like laundry. That, and helping my sister put up some shelves, are what my calendar looks like today."

"So you're an average man?"

"I hope to show you I'm better than average." He grinned, showing his dimples. "I have another three-day shift at the firehouse starting tomorrow, but maybe after that we could find some superhuman things to do together."

"I'm not bungee jumping. Ever."

"Okay, we'll paraglide instead."

Gail choked on her orange juice, and for a second was afraid it would spurt out through her nose. She decided to assume that he was joking.

It was nearly noon when Leon returned to his apartment complex. As he pulled into his parking spot, a familiar figure appeared next to the driver's side door. Resigning himself to confrontation, he stepped out onto the pavement, sighing.

"Karma."

"How could you, Leon?" Her eyes glittered with practiced tears. "You hurt me by not showing up yesterday. I told my mom you'd carve the turkey. You hurt my whole family."

"I told you I wasn't coming. I told your sister, too."

"How could you spend Thanksgiving with that bitch, Miss Frigid?"

"She's not, and her name's—" he broke off abruptly when he saw Karma zero in on his words like a hawk on a rabbit. The less Karma knew about her, the safer Gail would be. But how did she know where he was on Thanksgiving? Was she only guessing? Did she know he'd spent the night there, too?

A cunning smile played across Karma's lips. She flipped her long red hair over her shoulder. "You think I don't know who she is? I know everything about her."

He pressed his lips together, saying nothing.

She clasped her fingers around a handful of his sweater. "I'm trying to protect you from that harpy, Leo."

"Leon," he growled.

"I know you, lover. She doesn't. She's out to trap you."

He pulled her fingers away from his chest, but she quickly grasped his hand, saying, "Let's go inside. I'll make you forget about her."

"I'm not letting you in."

She pouted. "What if I bang on your door until you do?" She turned toward the building, tugging on his hand. "We could start on our decorating project."

Leon jerked his hand away and slid back into his SUV.

"Leo!" Karma fumbled in her purse as he started the engine and put the RAV4 into reverse.

As he backed out of the parking space, a shrill squeal accompanied the motion. Karma stood only inches away, holding her keys against the finish of the car, backing up only when he turned the wheel and threatened to run over her foot.

He stepped on the gas and peeled out of the parking lot. Shit, was he going to have to move to get rid of her? Would that even work? As he rounded the corner of the building, driving too fast, he nearly ran down a barrel-shaped man. In the rearview mirror, he saw the apartment manager squinting his eyes, frowning furiously in his direction.

Shit, shit, shit! He pounded on the steering wheel. He might not have a choice about moving.

Chapter 24

Leon couldn't visit for a few days, but he surprised Gail by asking a friend to install a security system and motion sensor lights at her house.

"I noticed you sometimes don't even turn your outdoor lights on when you leave," he told her. "I don't want to worry about you."

"I've never had a security system before."

"You always had . . . someone . . . living with you before."

The ghost of Terry rose up in her head. "True."

There was a brief hesitation on the other end of the phone, and then he said, "Now Charlie's over at Jon's most of the time." After another second of silence, he added, "This could keep graffiti off your garage door. It might even discourage the raccoons from raiding your garbage cans."

"Or just make them think they're on stage. I'm not worried. I have a guard cat now."

"I really want to do this, Gail," he insisted. "And put a decent lock on your back gate, too. I need to know you're safe."

"Maybe the raccoons will tap dance in the spotlight." She was joking, but the memory of the decapitated rat darkened her thoughts. Maybe motion sensor lights and a security system would discourage Orion from dismembering small mammals in the backyard. It was reassuring to think that someone wanted to protect her. "Okay, I agree, Leon, but I really should pay for everything."

"I'm getting a discount from this friend, but if you're truly concerned, I'm sure we can come up with a way for you to pay me back. I can think of multiple ways right now, as a matter of fact," he crooned in a husky voice.

"Ooh, can you now?" she responded, thinking of a few likely scenarios herself. She'd only been with Leon twice, but she was looking forward to future sessions in her bed. In any bed, for that matter. When it came to lovemaking, her soldier husband Keith had always been overeager on his rare homecomings. Mark, too, was daring but too fast. Terry was always considerate and sweet, willing to cuddle and kiss for as long as she wanted. But Leon—that man had the gift of *timing*. He could play her like a violin, beginning slow and mellow, working up to a tarantella tempo, and keeping her in suspense until she was practically ready to scream with ecstasy.

"Unfortunately, I'm at work. And a call—the professional equivalent of a cold shower—just came in, so I can't even fantasize about this any longer. The installer—his name is Ellis—will call you. Gotta run!"

She could hear the loudspeaker at the fire station in the background. "Bye. Thank you. Be careful."

Gail's new security system took a bit of getting used to. She taught Charlie and Elisa how to use the key codes, and in the next two days, Gail set the alarm off twice before she remembered to disarm it before walking into the house.

She wasn't sure she liked the motion sensor lights, either. Orion continued to insist on having the curtains open to the backyard, and sure enough, the lights flashed on when a raccoon strolled across the grass. The brightness didn't seem to discourage them. They simply sat back, their paws held up before their chests, blinking at the sudden spotlight. But they never managed to pry the bungee cord from the trash can.

Orion continued to warn her of nocturnal dangers. The second night after the new lights had been installed, he stood up, growling, at two a.m., and then ran into the living room just as the light flashed on out front, illuminating the porch.

Gail thought she heard footsteps, but that proved to be her imagination, because when she parted the curtains to survey the front yard, she saw nothing.

With some trepidation, she opened the front door. There was a small blob on the porch. She bent to study it closer, then quickly recoiled. It was the head of another rat. Orion sniffed at it. A small trail of blood led off the side of the porch, and the cat padded to the edge and stared off into the grass. Keeping her hand on the door frame, Gail took a step in that direction. The body of the rat lay beside the porch.

She stepped back into the doorframe. "So it's not you," she murmured.

The cat sat on his haunches and regarded her with his calm green stare. Was it her imagination, or did he look deeply offended?

"I'm sorry I accused you, buddy."

With a twitch of his tail, the cat leaped off the porch and vanished into the bushes. "Orion!" she called softly. "Can't you see it's not safe out there, you doofus? You've got five minutes to get back here, or you're spending the night out there!"

Before she went back into the house, she used the toe of her slipper to slide the rat head off the porch, grimacing. The blood showed it was a recent kill. A bobcat had been seen several times in the neighborhood over the past few years; she prayed it wasn't back. But it seemed bizarre that a wild creature would leave its prey on her porch.

Probably just another housecat, she told herself. She hoped Orion wasn't confronting any creature bigger and wilder than that.

Sleep was a long time coming. She tossed and punched her pillows, listening for the cat's meow. The thought that a light could flash on at any time was making her sleep less soundly instead of making her feel more secure.

When she checked the doors the next morning, Orion was not sitting outside. As she dressed for work, she told herself that the cat was visiting his previous home. But by the time she went to bed, Orion still had not come back.

Gail couldn't get the thought of the bobcat out of her brain. She didn't know whether her heart could take another loss, even if it was a cat she'd only just begun to care about.

When Leon crossed paths with the apartment manager the next morning, the man gave no indication that he remembered that Leon had nearly run him down. Maybe he hadn't noticed who was behind the wheel. Leon chose not to enlighten him and continued to his parking spot. Tucked under his windshield wiper was a single page of copier paper, a printout of a photo. The picture was grainy, either not taken with a good camera or not printed on a high-quality printer. Were those eyes peering out of the dark?

On the back of the page was the strange message *I'm working on it.*

What the hell? The note wasn't signed, but it had to come from Karma. Disgusted, he tossed the note into the back seat and drove to work.

Chapter 25

When Leon checked in with Gail the next day between EMT runs, she seemed preoccupied. "You're not worried about the trip, are you? Everything's all arranged. I can't wait."

"No, it's not that. I'm looking forward to that. You remember Orion?"

"Of course. Your cat. Has something happened to him?"

"I don't know. He disappeared in the middle of the night the day before yesterday. I can't find him anywhere."

"Did you let him out in the middle of the night?"

She told him about the security light flashing on and another dead rat and Orion running off. Then she said, "I went back to his old house, but nobody's seen him there. And the shelters don't have him. I called. I'm really worried that something, a bobcat or a coyote or even maybe a raccoon, got him."

"Oh, Gail, I'm so sorry. I've got another twelve hours to go here, but then I'll help you look for him tomorrow, okay? He might just haven gotten himself locked in someone's garage."

"Leon, I know you're busy. I didn't mean to burden you with my problems." She sounded sad.

"Your problems are my problems," he said. "See you tomorrow after work, okay?"

Unfortunately, the next EMT run involved an elderly woman who turned out to be a hoarder. Not only was her house filthy and stacked floor to ceiling with everything imaginable, but there were cats, dogs, and even rabbits everywhere. The woman had fallen down the narrow trail of open space that led down her stairs and broken her hip. There was not even room to bring the gurney into the house; they had to carry her outside, and as they did, Leon spotted several sets of frightened eyes peering out at them from dark holes between all the stacks of possessions. The old lady was in a lot of pain, but still coherent enough to cuss them out when they called the Humane Society and the police.

"I'm not going to get that smell out of my head for a while," Jon complained after they'd dropped their patient at the hospital.

"And all those eyes," Leon said.

"Yeah," his partner agreed. "That was creepy. Those poor animals."

"I'm gonna see those eyes in my sleep," Leon said. Dusk was quickly turning to darkness as he drove back to the station, and when the car in front of the aid truck braked, the two glowing red lights again reminded him of eyes. In his long career as a firefighter and paramedic, he'd seen a lot of things that he couldn't forget, but for some reason the glowing eyes seemed especially haunting.

Eyes.

A memory flashed into his tired brain.

As soon as Leon had parked the aid truck in the garage, Jon hopped out, saying, "I'll start the report."

"Thanks. I need to get something out of my car, and then I'll be in." He went out to his car, rummaged in the back seat, and pulled up the sheet of paper he'd found tucked under his windshield wiper two days before. Taking it into station house, he held the page under a lamp. Eyes. Rounded in fear. Behind some sort of gridwork that looked fuzzy in the copied photo. He sucked his lower lip between his teeth. Was that blur an ear? And those streaks, whiskers? Finally, he made up his mind that this could be a photo of a cat.

Gail's cat?

He felt nauseous as he pressed Karma's phone number into his phone.

"Lover!" she answered. "Feeling lonely? Do you want me to come over?"

"What did you do to the cat, Karma?"

"Cat? I don't know what you're talking about, Leo."

"Gail's cat."

"Is that the bitch's name?"

He didn't respond.

"She had a cat?"

The radio blared another call for both the engine and the aid truck for a multiple-vehicle traffic accident, and Leon hung up. It looked like it was going to be a long night.

He prayed Karma's use of the past tense was only a slip of the tongue. If she had killed Orion, he'd never forgive himself.

Chapter 26

The doorbell inside the townhouse chimed, and Leon shifted his weight nervously from foot to foot as he waited. Karma had texted him her address long ago, but he'd never been here before. For all he knew, it was another one of her lies. It wasn't even dawn yet. He wanted to surprise her, keep her off guard.

Karma, her hair in wild disarray and her body clad in only a loosely draped kimono wrap, pushed open the door. A devious smile played across her lips.

"Leo, lover," she purred, grabbing the front of Leon's rain jacket and pulling him toward her. "You've finally come to your senses."

He slapped at her hand. "The cat, Karma."

She blinked at him and pursed her lips, pouting. "I don't know what you're talking about." Then she stepped back and pulled the door open wider. "Come in."

Karma's living room was stunning. Blue and orange pillows were artfully arranged against a white leather couch, which were flanked by two blue armchairs with white pillows. A glass-topped coffee table reflected the light from an art deco lamp in the corner. There was not a magazine or a coffee cup or even a hair out of place.

"The cat," he reiterated. "What have you done with Gail's cat?"

Karma turned her head and lifted her chin and froze in what she probably thought was a movie-star pose. Then she swiveled back to look at him. "You mean the bitch you've been sniffing around? The bitch who's trying to trap you?"

He wanted to slap her, but instead fisted his hands at his sides. "Karma, Gail has never done anything to you. I love her—"

"You don't!" She slapped both hands against his chest and shoved him backward. "You don't, Leo, you don't! She's a bitch, she's convinced you that she needs you, but she's just using you." Flecks of spittle spattered Leon's cheeks, and he suddenly wished he'd had mediation training, or counseling, or something. The only guidance he could remember at the moment were lessons from a required course for all EMTs in how to deal with the mentally ill.

Treat them with respect. With kindness. Help them distinguish reality from delusions.

He gently took hold of her forearms. "Karma, look, I respect you, and I know you respect me, too. We're both adults here, right?"

Her posture softened. "Right, Leo. That's what I've been trying to get across to you. We belong together, the two of us." Leaning forward, she pressed her lips to his.

Leon had the urge to raise a hand and wipe his mouth, but he did his best not to even flinch. Should he play along, or confront her with reality? Confronting her did not seem to be working. "Maybe we do belong together, Karma. I was up all night, so maybe I'm not thinking straight. But first I need to sort things out with Gail. If you've done something to her cat—"

"I wouldn't have a cat in my house!" she protested. She broke away from him and positioned herself on the couch reclining against the cushions, one hand raised to her hair. "Look! My condo is immaculate. We're perfect, aren't we?"

Her white kimono was splashed with flowers in orange and blue. Karma matched her living room. Instead of being beautiful, the image was disturbing.

But maybe this was the angle he needed. "You—and this place—are gorgeous, Karma. What I don't understand is why you want me. Look at me. I'm a mess. My life's a mess. I would just mess up your perfect life. I don't want that for you."

She stood up. "But we can fix all that, Leo. When you're with me."

Shit. This wasn't working. "I can see the possibility, Karma."

"Ditch the bitch." Her eyes glittered with malice.

"Well, first I have to do something about the cat, Karma. You haven't killed the cat, have you?" Leon's heart clenched at the horrific thought.

"I don't know what you're talking about." Her posture softened. "But if a cat's disappeared, I can help you look for it. I wouldn't want anything to happen to a precious kitty. I love animals."

"Do you love rats?"

"What are you talking about? You're not making sense, Leo. Rats? Cats? I don't know what you're talking about."

He backed up toward the door. "Then I have no reason to talk to you."

Turning, he strode out the door, jerking it closed behind him. He sat in his RAV4, fuming, checked his watch. Damn Karma. He'd promised to be at his sister's in an hour. He knew Karma was lying. But he couldn't call the cops about a missing cat, could he? He had no evidence to prove Karma had killed those rats or taken Gail's cat.

He stared at the townhouse. Karma had the end unit with a one-car garage beside the front door. The curtains were pulled aside, and she glared at him from an upper window, letting her kimono fall open to reveal her breasts.

I wouldn't have a cat in my house.

Putting the SUV in gear, he drove a short distance down the street, then parked and walked back. He tried Karma's garage door. Locked. It would be nearly impossible to jimmy that without getting noticed by anyone driving by. He walked to the side of the garage and tried the lock on the small door there. As a fireman, he'd had a fair amount of experience picking locks and breaking door frames when that didn't work. Fortunately, this flimsy lock was not a deadbolt, and gave way easily enough when he applied the tension wrench that most of the fire station crew carried to let themselves into homes when the occupants were in no condition to come to the door.

No alarm sounded. He flicked on the light switch. He might have only seconds before Karma came to check. "Kitty, kitty," he called softly.

A faint meow came from a set of shelves in front of the white Subaru. Thank God. Between boxes labeled Christmas Decorations was a gray cat carrier. A dirty cat stared out at him from the grillwork on the front door. The creature was filthy and looked miserable. Sticking a paw through the mesh, the cat meowed again. Orion.

Gripping the cat carrier, he pulled it from the shelf just as the door from the garage into the condo opened. He ran for the exterior door, slammed it behind him, heard Karma furiously shouting "Leo!" as he jogged down the street to his SUV.

Gail was thrilled when he delivered the cat. "I spotted him a couple of neighborhoods over during a call."

"Oh, thank you, thank you, thank you, Leon! You're my hero!" She wrapped her arms around him.

Leon didn't feel like a hero. He was a coward and a liar.

"You can keep the carrier. It's an extra." He couldn't bear to tell Gail the mortifying truth about Karma. But now he had proof that Karma not only knew who Gail Langston was but also had visited her house several times. He was determined to fix the situation as soon as he could.

Chapter 27

After consulting with Donovan Kelly, Leon knew he needed to file for a civil antiharassment order. That was apparently the terminology to discourage a stalker who wasn't a spouse or family member. Donovan didn't bother to stifle his snicker when Leon began to explain about this sexy babe who was pursuing him, but as he heard more about Karma's actions, the police officer grew more sympathetic.

"It happens," he told Leon. "Stalkers are more often men than women, but there have been workplace shooters who are stalkers of both genders. The law doesn't do a very good job of protecting against them. And you never know what a stalker might pull next."

With metal detectors and marble floors and high ceilings at its entry, the district courthouse felt at first like an intimidating space. Fortunately, the offices inside were more common looking, and the woman in the district court clerk's office was nice enough. She was no doubt used to helping both accusers and accused navigate the paperwork of the court system.

"Have you had this person charged before?" she asked, her pen poised over the form she was helping him fill out. Then, when Leon hesitated, she clarified, "Would there be police records or a court history of problems between you?"

"No," he said. "Although I probably should have had her arrested for breaking and entering into my apartment and destroying my property. And for kidnapping my friend's cat."

The clerk didn't comment on that, but summarized by saying, "So it's not an emergency situation. You're not in immediate bodily danger?"

"Guess not." The woman's no-nonsense attitude was starting to make him feel foolish.

He'd have to appear before a judge to explain the situation, she told him, and the respondent would be notified in the meantime.

"Respondent?" Leon asked.

"The person you're asking for protection from. That person has a right to appear before the judge at the same hearing."

Leon grimaced. Great. He'd hoped that Karma would simply receive an official order to stay away from him, and that she'd obey. Now he'd have to face her in a courtroom? Was there no end to this humiliating situation? He couldn't believe he was in this position. He respected women, he'd always tried to be decent to April and Stacey at the station and Marina while on volunteer duty, even being careful never to say disparaging things about girls to his little nieces. And he'd been respectful to Karma in the beginning, too. She had definitely encouraged him in that bar where they'd met. But he had no way to prove that.

Bite the bullet, he told himself, sighing. Karma's behavior had to stop, and he couldn't exactly shoot her, could he? Plus, he worried that since Karma clearly knew where Gail lived, she might go after Gail herself. "I also need to add another person's name to the protection order," he told the clerk.

"Unless it's a minor in your custody, that person will also have to appear in court to explain to the judge."

Oh God. Then he'd have to describe the whole embarrassing situation to Gail, and she'd have to be in the courtroom with Karma, too, and God only knows what the lunatic might say. Karma was so good at convincing others that *she* was the victim. He was getting a headache just thinking about the potential scene.

"The hearing will be"—the clerk checked her schedule—"right after Christmas holiday, say, on December twenty-seventh?"

Right in the middle of their Roatan trip. He shook his head. "No, I won't be in town then."

"No problem. What date will you be available?" The woman picked up her pen.

He told her. After writing it down, she asked, "Do you want to add that second person's information now?"

"No, I guess not." He hoped that Karma would receive the notification of their court date while he and Gail were out of town, and then the whole ugly situation would quietly resolve itself before they returned. He paid the filing fee and left the building, feeling as if he needed a stiff drink, although it was only eleven o'clock in the morning.

Chapter 28

Between Thanksgiving and their scheduled trip, Leon stayed over a few times, but he was taking all the overtime he could get to build up his savings account. Charlie had practically moved in with Jon. So Gail was doubly grateful for Jeannie's friendship and for Orion's company in the evenings. If Leon hadn't spotted the cat, Orion might have ended up in the animal shelter or in some stranger's home.

When he was with her on his days off, Leon seemed preoccupied, and Gail started to fret that he might be regretting inviting her along on the scuba trip. After all, she was a total rookie; all his friends were expert divers. Would she be a drag on the whole group? Would she be able to keep up? He assured her she already fit in just fine with the group, and he repeatedly showed her that she fit into his arms perfectly, too.

She didn't have an opportunity to go diving again, but she swam almost every day after work to build up her stamina, and the regularity of swimming often made her think of other rhythms. The memory of their lovemaking could make a flush creep outward from her most intimate places, and she felt her face grow hot even in the cool water of the pool. It was almost embarrassing to think how much she was looking forward to spending a week sharing a room with him in the tropics.

But every time she glimpsed the photos of Terry on the kitchen wall, she felt a twinge of guilt. Elisa was envious of the trip, so close to Guatemala, the country of her mother. Charlie, however, still seemed to believe that Gail shouldn't even entertain the idea of scuba diving, let alone having hot sex with Leon in an exotic locale. Christmas, she reminded her mother, was usually one of the best sales times for florists. So the thought of leaving her struggling shop didn't sooth her conscience, either. The physical exertion of swimming was a nice break from her mental anxieties about the business and this new relationship with Leon.

"So what if it doesn't last forever?" Jeannie reminded Gail as they worked on creating stars and fairies and Santa Clauses and angels to add to Christmas bouquets. "Aren't you having a good time with Leon?"

Gail blushed. "Yes." She'd already confessed a few intimate details to her friend.

"Aren't you looking forward to the trip? Starry nights under warm tropical skies, a hot fire department EMT in your bed? Scuba diving with rainbow fish and dancing the nights away. How can you entertain a shred of doubt for even a second?"

"Well—"

"Well, you are total dingbat doofus if you do. And by the way . . ." She wheeled herself to the chest of drawers that held art supplies and pulled a package from the lowest drawer. "Here. Early Christmas present."

It was a beautiful sarong, soft silky rayon with an orange-and-gold-and-black batik pattern.

"Wow."

"Find a sexy swim suit to match."

"I think I have a black one. If it still fits. I only wore it once, when Terry and I went to California before . . ." Oh God, why did she have to start down that road again? She swallowed and continued. "It has a strip of mesh that goes diagonally across here." She drew a line from her left hip that crossed between her breasts to her right shoulder.

"Find it."

Gail fingered the soft fabric of the sarong. "But I have nothing for you."

Jeannie made a scoffing noise and leaned on the work table, grinding glitter into her forearm. "The only Christmas present I want from you is to hear all the scandalous details about your amazing trip."

Gail held up her hands in surrender. "Okay, okay! Now, stop calling me a dingbat doofus. Thanks, girlfriend."

"You're welcome, dorkhead." Jeannie waved a fairy wand in Gail's direction. "Now go out and play."

A wing fell off the fairy, and Gail stared at it in dismay. An omen? "See what can happen?"

Jeannie dabbed a bit of glue onto the fairy's back and pressed the wing back into place. "See how easily it can be fixed? Like magic."

Chapter 29

Like the others in the circle, Gail knelt in her scuba gear on the sandy sea bottom in front of the Coco View Resort, dreading what was to come next. The plane had touched down only three hours ago, and her anxiety was ratcheting up by the minute. The Honduran divemaster had demanded that everyone prove basic skills. Gail hadn't had a chance to dive again after her first open-water test, and she knew she'd never measure up to the experienced scuba divers who surrounded her. Her own heartbeat filled her ears. Aside from that, she heard only her own breathing and a few odd metallic clicks now and then.

She twisted her head to gaze at Leon kneeling beside her. Through his mask, his calm gray eyes crinkled at the corners with the laugh lines she loved. He was smiling. He slowly closed, then opened his right eye, winking at her. Reaching out, he took her hand, trying to reassure her. In the underwater gloom, his silvery hair looked almost snow white, and the skin of their joined hands was ghostly pale. With his free hand, he gave her an OKAY sign.

Was she crazy to have joined him in Roatan? This was the first time she'd be away from home at Christmas since she'd married Terry more than twenty-five years ago, and she felt guilty for enjoying a vacation instead of exchanging presents and cooking for her family. She should be back in her safe flower shop, tucking miniature Santas and sequined stars and poinsettias into beribboned bouquets for Christmas, not breathing compressed air from tanks in a tropical ocean. When she'd first pulled on her old swimsuit, she'd found another of Terry's notes pinned inside: *Whoa, baby!*

Her husband had meant it as a compliment, she knew, but on first reading, the note seemed more like a warning: *Whoa, baby! Stop, now!*

Leon, despite his assurances that he was not always a thrill seeker, had probably been born as fearless as the lion he was named for. He was the first man to believe that she could be fearless, too. But now her stomach was churning, and the idea of bolting seemed almost irresistible.

When the black-clad man in the center of the circle pointed his index finger at her, Leon dropped her hand. Her turn. Her own breath sounded like strangled gurgling now, and her heart had somehow climbed into her sinuses. She glanced quickly at Leon again.

He crossed his arms against his chest, the sign for *I love you*. Right now, the gesture reminded her more of a corpse with crossed arms than a sign of affection.

Buck up, Gail Langston. You've done this before. Time to show you're not the fragile orchid in this tropical flower arrangement. She gulped, swallowing down her panic, then slipped off her scuba mask. Everything in front of her became a gray blur. Saltwater stabbed her eyes. Grabbing blindly for the strap, she stretched it down over her hair and pushed the mask back onto her face, holding it with her hands. Exhaling heavily through her nose, she puffed air into the mask. Her eyes and nostrils smarted from the salt, but the water exited through the top skirting, just like it was supposed to, followed by air bubbles that streamed through her bangs.

She glanced at her lover again. Leon made a clapping motion. She doubted that she deserved applause for that basic maneuver, but she made the crossed-arm sign back to him. He nodded briefly before ripping off and then replacing his own mask.

She'd caught a lock of her ash-blond hair inside the skirting of her mask, and drips of seawater steadily dribbled from it now, snaking down the inside of her mask to form a pool under her nostrils. Rubbing her fingers across her forehead, she fingered out the strand and pressed her mask tighter against her face.

A cloud of tiny cobalt fish flitted between the neoprene-clad participants, zipping away as the divemaster flapped his hands to dismiss the circle of divers, motioning them toward the buoys marking the underwater path back to the beach resort.

Leon touched her arm, and then raised a hand to point to the bright orb of the late-afternoon sun shining through the thirty feet of water overhead. A kite shape flew across the spotlight, its long tail swishing behind. An eagle ray. She'd seen a photo in her identification program. It was amazing to see such an otherworldly creature in the flesh.

She put both thumbs up, then remembered that was the signal to surface, and she clapped her hands together instead to celebrate the sight of the ray. Then they turned to follow the others back to the beach through the boulders and coral castles and waving sea grass. Tomorrow would be soon enough to see more of the Caribbean marine life. After the long flight today and now the tense drills, Gail welcomed a relaxing glass of wine and dinner overlooking the bay.

Thanks to Leon, she was now a scuba diver. She had romance and adventure and hot sex again in her life. For once, Charlie and Elisa had good reason to be envious of her, instead of the other way around.

Now, if only she could convince her fireman to settle for all this fun, this romance and adventure and passion, she could relax and enjoy her new life.

But she had the disturbing suspicion that Leon wanted even more.

Chapter 30

The first day of diving at Coco View was a busy blur of introductions to their divemasters and their boat and safety procedures. They were assigned to a boat with Leon's five friends and two other vacationing couples. Gail was nervous as they motored out of the sheltered resort bay and then tied up to a mooring ball only about fifteen minutes away.

Out in this open area, the wind was blowing. Waves rocked the boat, and she worried about falling off the stern when it was her turn to stagger up off the bench with her heavy tank on her back and waddle to the open platform with her fins on. Guillermo, the boat driver, sensed her anxiety and held her arm as they proceeded. He tested her tank valve to be sure it was open, and then peered into her facemask. "Okay?"

Placing her mouthpiece between her lips, she took a breath. Although they'd practiced the giant stride off the side of the pool in class, she'd never jumped off a boat before.

"Ready?"

She looked to her right. Leon winked at her from behind his mask.

She nodded, afraid to remove her mouthpiece to speak.

"Then let's do it!" He shoved his mouthpiece between his lips, put a hand over his mask, and leaped off the stern into the waves.

When he bobbed up and tapped his head to signal he was okay, she copied his form and leaped off. Unlike the waters of Puget Sound, the Caribbean was warm, but when she bobbed up, the bouncing of the wind-driven waves threatened to make her nauseous. She was eager to let the air out of her buoyancy control vest—BC, for short—and descend into the quieter water below.

Leon swam below her, rolling onto his back now and then to signal, *Okay?* Making her index finger and thumb into a circle, she signaled back that she was. She checked her dive computer and air gauge several times to be sure they were working. Then she finally relaxed enough to study her surroundings as she drifted downward. She was proud when she remembered to add air to her BC to keep from crashing onto the fauna and flora covering the ocean floor.

When she stopped kicking and paddling with her arms, she could simply stay in place, suspended in the water. Amazing. This was how Keith must have felt while flying his helicopter.

A school of neon-blue fish flitted through orange and yellow corals. An incredible striped parrotfish ripped off chunks of an unlucky sponge. Garden eels vanished into their holes in the sand as the divers passed over the plateau. Anemones and sea fans waved in the gentle current as she and Leon dropped over the edge of a wall to follow the divemaster and the rest of the group.

As they discovered living treasures, they signaled to each other and passed the information down the line. Wiggling fingers indicated a giant lobster waving his long antennae from a crevice. A pinching motion could be either a crab or a shrimp. In some cases, Gail couldn't tell the difference, there were so many types. Tiny red-and-white creatures that might have been either; big orange, squat monsters that were clearly crabs; translucent, miniature animals with neon stripes that didn't look like anything she'd seen before.

The divemaster honked his air horn, calling everyone's attention, and then made a motion like a kid riding a hobbyhorse. Sure enough, he'd located a tiny seahorse, its tail wrapped around a coral branch. She wondered what the creature thought about these bubbling giants crowding around to study it.

The dive was over too soon. They slowly ascended and leveled off for a safety stop. Leon held out his arms as if to say, "Well, what did you think?"

Gail clapped her hands slowly together to show her appreciation. Then over Leon's shoulder, she caught a glimpse of sleek shapes in the distance. She pointed. Leon swiveled around in time to watch three rays swimming in formation into the blue gloom. Then it was his turn to clap.

Her dive computer dinged to signal the end of the safety-stop timer, and they surfaced together. Hanging onto a hinged dive ladder that bobbed in the waves while she removed her fins was a challenge, but Gail was proud of herself when she managed the task without dropping a fin or slipping off the rungs.

When they were seated on the boat again, the group of friends began discussing the underwater terrain.

"Man, that reef is not how I remembered it from last year," Donovan remarked.

Stacey took a gulp from her water bottle. "Didn't there used to be a huge purple barrel sponge here on the lip of the wall?"

Guillermo overheard the conversation. "There was a big rockslide from the *terremoto*," he told them. He frowned, repeating, "*Terremoto*?"

"Earthquake," Donovan translated.

When they all turned curious faces his way, Guillermo explained further. "We have a earthquake last March. *Muy fuerte.* Strong. It breaks many water lines on Roatan, and— how you say—slide of rocks under the water." Then, noting their concerned expressions, he added, "But for luck, it happens at night. Nobody is hurt. All is normal now."

"I didn't know they had earthquakes here," April said.

"*Sí. El plato del Caribe.*" He glanced at Donovan.

"The . . . er . . . Caribbean plate?" he guessed.

Guillermo jabbed his index finger at Donovan. "*Exacto.* But not to worry. *Un terremoto* is *muy raro,* rare." Then one of the deckhands hailed him, and he strode back to the cabin.

"Caribbean plate, who knew?" Leon shrugged. They were all from Washington State and accustomed to living in the so-called Ring of Fire, the line of volcanoes and faults along the Pacific coastlines. "I guess you don't have to live near a volcano to have earthquakes."

Gail wondered how the marine life had behaved during the quake. Did fish panic when their world shook?

On the way back to the resort, she was surprised when the boat suddenly slowed and the experienced divers began to zip their wetsuits again and shrug back into their BCs with their attached tanks.

"We always swim along one of the walls back to the resort," Stacey explained.

"C'mon, you'll love it," Leon urged. He motioned for the divemaster to switch Gail's gear to a fresh air cylinder.

Gail longingly eyed the short distance back to the resort. She'd been looking forward to a shower and a cold drink, not to jumping into the ocean again less than an hour after she'd survived the last dive.

Conrad stuck his elbows out and flapped them like wings. "*Buck, buck, buck . . .*"

Nobody was going to call her a chicken. Pushing her arms into her BC, she tightened the straps. "Let's go."

Striding off the stern was easier this time, and after sinking down to the top of the wall, she did her best to copy Leon's slow and graceful froglike kick to move gently forward along the vertical rock face.

Newman's Wall to her left was covered in corals and sea fans, and full of lobsters and crabs, attended by striped and spotted fish of all colors. There was even one of the invasive lionfish lurking beneath a shelf. Gail knew they were native to the far Pacific, not the Caribbean, and renowned for multiplying like rabbits and devouring all the native fish. The dive guides at Coco View had pledged to kill every lionfish they saw, but she was glad this one had escaped their notice so she could see it. The lionfish was a spectacular creature, zebra-striped in brown and white, with ragged skin flags flying from the arrays of venomous spikes that jutted out from its body. It sailed through the water like a miniature pirate galleon, confident that no larger fish would attack it.

When Leon pointed down, Gail dipped her head to see a green moray snaking along the bottom of the wall below. It looked to be at least six feet long and nearly a foot thick. Had she seen such a serpentlike animal on land, she probably would have wet her pants. Here, in this otherworldly environment, it was another fascinating alien that breathed water instead of air.

By the time they reached the marker buoy at the end of the wall, Gail felt at ease with the other divers. When she checked her dive computer, she had nearly 1000 psi of air left. They turned and swam toward the wreck that dominated the bottom of the bay in front of Coco View. Swimming over it, Leon surprised a turtle that launched itself from between the streaming plants growing on the deck of the sunken ship.

They slowly followed Stacey, Conrad, and April up the sloping channel to the resort, decompressing as they went. Finally, they stood in waist-deep water to shed their fins. Gail was relieved to spit out her mouthpiece and pull the dive mask to the top of her head, and even happier to shrug out of her BC and deposit the heavy cylinder on the bench on shore.

Leon grinned at her, his eyes bright, sunlight glinting off the water in his silver hair. "First thoughts?"

She stood up, flexed her arms in a strongman pose. "I am

woman, see me dive!"

He laughed and threw his arms around her. "My wild woman! I knew you'd love it."

Chapter 31

Leon had warned her that Coco View was not a flashy resort. Gail enjoyed the laid-back ambience of the place. The manager had been very apologetic as he explained that the resort's internet connection was currently nonfunctional, but most of the guests seemed content to be incommunicado with life back home. The absence of electronic devices made the environment seem even more tranquil.

Between dives, Leon was happy to lounge in a hammock or go for a walk with her among the exotic flowers and coconut palms, following the paths of hummingbirds and iguanas. At night, bats took the place of the hummingbirds at the feeders outside the dining hall, and they both enjoyed watching the small winged mammals extending their long tongues to lap at the nectar.

Christmas was marked by fireworks on the evening before and then on Christmas day, by tamales and a special dessert, a sponge cake soaked in cream called *Tres Leches*. Gail gave Leon the latest science fiction thriller novel. He laughed when he unwrapped it and handed her a mystery novel.

Entertainment was local and casual. Pool and dancing in the bar most evenings. Tonight, crab races. Each diver paid a dollar to bet on a land crab of his or her choice, and the winner took the pot. When the bucket came around to her as she was enjoying a margarita after dinner, Gail picked the biggest crab left, a tan-colored brute with the number 14 painted on its back in red fingernail polish. To her surprise, Leon picked a small gray one, number 9.

"My crab could eat your crab," Gail joked.

He grinned. "That's why mine is going to run really fast."

"Crabs can run?"

"Scuttle? Scrabble? Crabble?"

They both laughed.

The racing rink was a rope circle in the sand. All the guests gathered around as one of the resort staff carefully decanted the crabs from their bucket into the middle of the circle, then uprighted the ones that landed on their backs, while another staff member corralled the crabs that were already trying to escape. They pushed the reluctant contestants together under a plastic dishpan, and then the countdown began. "*Uno, dos . . .*"

"*Tres!*" everyone shouted together as Guillermo lifted the dishpan.

Pandemonium erupted around the circle, with all the guests encouraging their racers.

"Go, Brutus, go!" Gail yelled. Number 14 crouched immobile, squatting exactly where he'd landed when dumped from the bucket. "Move it, you lazy lunkhead!"

Leon raised a brow at her. "Brutus?"

"Gotta be a guy crab," Gail explained.

He leaned over the rope. "Nine, they all want to EAT you! Run! Run!"

His tiny gray racer dashed toward the perimeter. But number 9 was not alone. On the other side of the circle, a medium-sized purplish crab—number 3—and a bigger brown one—15—were also scuttling toward the rope.

The shouting rose in volume.

"Fourteen!" Gail yelled. "Move!"

Finally, her crab shifted sideways a few inches, then hunkered down again. "Argh!" she groaned.

"Go, Nine, go, go, go, you beautiful girl!"

It was Gail's turn to give him a quizzical look.

Number 3 was in the lead, and the shrill cheers from his backer—a brunette from Dallas—threatened to pierce Gail's left eardrum. But then, number 3, perhaps catching sight of the rope blocking the way ahead, began to move sideways, back toward the center of the circle.

"No, no, no!" the brunette yelped.

"Nine, you can do it!" Leon's voice was loud in her right ear. "Bring it home!"

Gail contemplated throwing a rock at number 14. Brutus clearly needed motivation.

Then tiny gray 9 reached the rope. Leon straightened, thrusting both arms up in victory. "Wahoo!"

Everyone clapped good-naturedly, and Guillermo plopped the bucket full of dollar bills at Leon's feet. Leon stooped, plucked number 9 from the ground, and planted a kiss on the crab's tiny body. "Yeah, baby, I knew you were a winner when I saw you."

Gail folded her arms, chuckling. "I'm jealous."

"You don't need to be." His eyes twinkling with laughter, he set the crab down on the ground. "Now that I'm a wealthy man, I can make all my dreams come true."

He bent one knee to the sand. Gail thought he was going to gather the money from the bucket, but instead he turned toward her. "Gail Grace Langston."

The crowd hushed.

Leon whipped a small case from the pocket of his shorts. He popped it open. A diamond ring gleamed from its black satin background. "Would you do me the honor of becoming my wife?"

A shiver ran down her spine, a mix of excitement, pleasure. And terror.

Time seemed to stand still as she met Leon's eyes. His gaze was serene, happy. Hopeful.

Leon Maxwell was funny. He was kind. He was strong. He was compassionate. He worked hard, he played hard, he was a loyal friend and companion. He was brave. He was fun.

Gail felt the eyes of every guest on her. They were all waiting, silent, holding their collective breath.

Inside her head, her thoughts were screaming. Terry was supposed to be her last major decision, her final, happily-ever-after "Yes." But here was the chance to be happy again, kneeling before her, his blue-gray eyes fixed on her face. She wanted him. She knew she shouldn't take the chance. The two conflicting ideas batted her emotions back and forth like a ping-pong ball.

Leon bounced his eyebrows twice, and she couldn't help but laugh. She was tired of thinking so much. She could no longer deny it; she loved this man.

"Of course I will," she said.

The whole resort cheered.

Chapter 32

Their last evening of their scheduled trip in Roatan was a warm, windless night on the beach, with waves lapping gently on the shore. The other members of their party were dancing in the bar. Gail gazed longingly in that direction, but she'd promised to accompany Leon on a night dive. This would be her first nocturnal exploration, and although she was hesitant to duck beneath the dark water, she clamped her teeth around her mouthpiece and lowered her head into the cool sea. She was pleased to discover that, although they needed their dive lights to reveal the vivid colors of the reef, the underwater environment wasn't nearly as black as she'd feared. The full moon shone through the water. She was reassured by the bright orb when she looked up toward the glittering surface overhead.

She tried to concentrate on her breathing. Slow, deep. Relax. But she hadn't been truly relaxed since Leon's proposal. How could she have said yes? Last night she'd dreamed of uniformed men walking up to her door. Now she couldn't remember whether they'd been wearing military uniforms or police gear or maybe even fire department uniforms, but she'd known their approach could only mean one thing.

One moment her stomach was churning with anxiety, the next she was aglow with happiness and oh so eager to share her future with Leon Maxwell. All the resort guests and staff kept slapping Leon on the back and congratulating her, asking to see the incredible ring he'd given her. One moment she was telling herself that she was the luckiest woman alive to have found love for the fourth time. And then seconds later, she was remembering how three of those loves had ended abruptly and horribly.

Shit. She shook her head to get rid of those ugly thoughts. Focus. You're in a beautiful place with a beautiful man. And most importantly, you are twenty-five feet below the surface of the ocean. Be here, be now. She searched the dark water for Leon, located him up ahead by the beam of his dive light.

Leon was right, night diving proved to be a whole new experience. The fish, so abundant in the daylight, seemed largely absent until she studied the environment. They had parked themselves in rocky crevices, nestled inside of sponges and wedged into the fingers of corals. The water wasn't empty, though; the beam of her dive light revealed swarms of tiny worms and what looked like glowing beetles. The ocean floor slithered and crawled, too. Giant striped lobsters and dozens of shrimp paraded across the sand.

Instead of heading for the wreck, Leon turned left to swim along Coco View Wall, and they moved slowly along it. Leon pointed out a giant green moray lying on a narrow rock shelf. The snakelike animal seemed to glare at them for a moment as it slowly opened and closed its sharp-toothed mouth, forcing water through its gills, and then it undulated away into the darkness. A few feet away, Gail was startled by a gleaming eye in a crevice, and when she looked closer, she jerked backward in alarm. Leon joined her, flashing his light into the crevice. Then he turned and put his hand upright on top of his head.

Scuba sign language for shark. Leon made the usual clapping gesture, congratulating her on spotting the predator there. Nurse sharks, she'd been told, were harmless to divers. But adrenaline junkies were prone to saying things like that. The creature did not seem inclined to move, so they swam on instead, but Gail kept glancing back in the shark's direction to be sure it wasn't following them. She nearly ran straight into Leon's fins, and had to backpaddle at the last moment. He was so focused on a speckled creature moving through the coral that he didn't even notice.

The creature oozed in and out of the heads of corals and lumps of sponges, changing colors and patterns as it went. A small octopus, the first she'd seen, and clearly on the hunt. The sight was fascinating, and they both focused their lights on its progress. The octopus melted into impossible shapes to fit into narrow tubes. It threaded itself through the coral only to emerge a foot away and morph back into eight arms and a head. Its skin changed from a deep rose color to white and then sea green with bluish arms. Finally, the creature burrowed into a shallow cave, where it settled and changed its pattern to a mottled brown, blending into the surroundings. Leon pressed his head inside the cave to follow it.

Gail was getting cold. When she checked her dive computer, she was a bit alarmed to see they'd been down for fifty minutes. She had only 700 PSI left. In Seattle, the instructor had lectured them never to surface with less than 500, because air gauges were not precise measuring devices, and you never knew what could happen until you were safely out of the water.

She tapped Leon's arm, and when he turned in her direction, she showed him her air gauge, pressing the button to light it. He nodded and showed her his, which registered only 600. She gestured back the way they'd come. He held up his hand, thumb, and finger a short distance apart, which she interpreted as, *Just a little longer*. Turning back to the octopus, he held out a finger toward it. The creature reached out and gently touched Leon's finger with the pointed tip of its tentacle.

Gail understood that it was a magical moment, but they needed to get back. She glanced up. Through the smooth surface overhead, the moon looked reassuring.

Then, as she watched, the glasslike water shimmered into sharp-edged crystal shards, and she both heard and felt a deep rumble. A boat engine? Sudden turbulence bounced her into the wall, and she had to thrust out her hands to keep from bashing her head.

Debris showered down from above, and she instinctively back-paddled out of the rockfall. Had a boat plowed into the top of the reef above them?

The turbulence was making her nauseous. She fought to keep her regulator in place as a large chunk of coral tumbled down, striking her in the forehead. It bounced off and hit Leon in the back of the calf on its way to the bottom. The octopus shot out of the crevice. As Leon began to back out, Gail heard a loud crack, and she watched in horror as the crevice collapsed and the rock crashed onto her fiancé's arm. Even with his mouthpiece in place, she heard Leon's panicked shout, and at the same time she realized she was screaming through her own regulator.

Then the rumble silenced and the shaking lessened. The seawater no longer felt like a washing machine. Leon's eyes were wide under his facemask, but he held up his right hand, thumb and forefinger in a circle. Asking her if she were okay.

The thought, *Earthquakes are rare, my ass,* flashed irreverently through Gail's brain. She quickly signaled the "okay" sign back, then pointed to his arm. He pointed to himself and flashed the sign again.

She didn't believe that for a second. No way was Leon okay.

Pressing his free right hand against the rock face, he tried to pull out his left hand. It didn't move even a fraction of an inch, as far as she could see. She wedged her fingertips into the narrow crack beside his arm and tried to lift the rock that had collapsed onto him.

Nothing moved. She thrashed against the wall, trying to find purchase somewhere for her feet. It was impossible. There was no way to get leverage.

Oh God oh God oh God. They were fifty feet below the surface. Did anyone even know they were here? She picked up Leon's computer. The arrow in his air gauge was in now the red zone. Only 200 PSI. Hers registered 300. Sweet Jesus, Leon was going to die here.

She stared at his face. His eyes looked serene now, his expression resigned. He pressed his free arm against his chest and pointed to her. A one-handed *I Love You*. She crossed her arms and signed it back. Then he pointed back toward the resort and wiggled his fingers. *Goodbye.*

She shook her head violently. No. She couldn't let this happen. She couldn't let Leon die alone.

There was only one thing she could think of to do. It was the only chance. Reaching down, she unbuckled her BC. Leon shook his head and again gestured toward the resort. Ignoring him, she slipped her arms out of the vest.

His sounds of protest were loud as she slid out of the buoyancy vest with its attached air cylinder. Her body began to float upward almost immediately, and she yanked one of the lead weights out of a BC pocket to help. Awkwardly, holding the weight in one hand, she slid the other shoulder strap of her BC over Leon's free arm.

He violently shook his head, and through the facemask, his eyes beseeched her to stop. She took a final deep breath from her regulator, then took it out of her mouth and tucked the mouthpiece beneath the shoulder strap of Leon's BC, next to his neck. Her gaze glued to his, she pressed her fingers to her lips and then waved in his direction, giving him a watery kiss.

Chapter 33

Gail kicked and began ascending toward the surface, keeping hold of the weight in her hand. She tried to rise slowly, exhaling as she went, dribbling air bubbles from her lips just like she'd practiced in the pool during training. But this wasn't fifteen feet of water, it was fifty.

The moonlit surface seemed impossibly far away; her lungs burned long before she dropped the weight and broke through into air. Finally, with her face in the night air, she gasped desperately, coughing and trying to catch her breath. The waves at the surface were violent, slapping against her face. She sucked in a gulp of salt water and coughed more. Her head was spinning. It seemed as if there wasn't enough oxygen in the world.

Help. She had to get help. Leon was trapped and running out of air. Onshore, the buildings were dark. Trees whipped back and forth in an insane hula. Only splashes of light darted around—flashlights. She heard shouting in Spanish and English, all mixed together. *Terremoto! Temblor!* Earthquake!

Another tremor passed through the water, and as she watched, onshore a palm crashed to the ground. An aftershock? *Oh God.* More rocks might be tumbling down on Leon this very instant, crushing him, burying him.

"Help!" she screamed, treading water between the choppy waves. "Help!"

Surf crashed against the shallow reef between her and the shore. Her voice was too small, and the few cottages she could see were too far away. Flipping onto her stomach, she put her snorkel into her mouth and her face into the water and swam for all she was worth toward the dock at Coco View Resort.

The wave action was even more violent on top of the shallow reef, tossing her like a rag doll, slamming her into the corals. Her whole body was on fire from their stings. It seemed like it took forever to drag herself into the swim channel.

Finally, through the silty water, she saw the vertical shadows that were the pilings of the dock. Lifting her face from the water, she searched for someone; anyone. "Help!"

Her throat was too dry; she couldn't shout loud enough.

The moon had gone behind a cloud. Everything was too dark.

"Help!" she screamed, struggling to pull off her fins.

Her shout was drowned by the generator finally kicking on. Lights flared and the music started up again. A group of guests streamed out of the main lodge building onto the dock.

"Help!" she shouted. "Help me! Help!" What was the Spanish? "*Ayudo!* Help!"

Finally, they looked in her direction, shielding their eyes from the overhead lights, searching the water. Stacey. Diego, their divemaster. She waved frantically. "Leon's trapped underwater!"

Stacey and Diego turned away and vanished into the shadows toward the equipment shed. What the hell? Hadn't they understood her? "Leon's trapped!" she screamed after them. "He's out of air!"

A man dove into the water and surfaced beside her. "Where?"

He was one of the young men who worked filling their air tanks; she thought his name might be Armando.

"Coco View Wall," she told him. "Fifty feet down. Somewhere in front of the beach houses. I'll show you."

Two divers dashed into the water beside her, Stacey and

the divemaster, dressed in T-shirts and shorts but with masks on their heads, tanks and fins strapped on, and dive lights in hand.

"We need leverage," Gail told them. "His arm is trapped."

Footsteps thundered on the dock and then a boat hook and a long metal rod splashed in the water beside them. Grabbing the rod, Stacey ducked underwater and began to swim.

"I need a tank," Gail gasped at the two men near her. The other diver shook his head and shoved his regulator into his mouth, then vanished underwater.

Armando tried to take her hand, but she slipped away, and ran after the divers until the water was up to her chin. "Save him!" she screamed.

The world seemed lopsided and half-crimson. Gail wiped at her right eye. Blood streamed from a cut on her forehead. That falling rock.

Leon was going to die. The curse had followed her all the way to Honduras. Because she had promised to marry him? If she really loved him, she would have said no.

Behind her, the generator throbbed unevenly, causing the lights to blink off and on again. Seawater rippled around her. The full moon emerged from the clouds and began to wobble in the sky, and then spin in crazy circles.

And then the whole world went black.

Chapter 34

Leon stared longingly at the dive light lying on the sea bottom twenty feet below his fins. It would have been nice to be able to at least enjoy the underwater scenery before he died in the dark depths, maybe spot a colorful fish or two for the last time. Gail had been incredibly brave and cool-headed for a newbie diver. He was so proud of her. As he'd watched her swim away, he prayed she had not given herself the bends with that too-fast emergency ascent.

Abruptly, his trachea stuck halfway through a breath. Even though he'd been expecting to run out of air, panic shot through his brain at the inability to fill his lungs. Holding his breath, he spit out his mouthpiece, exchanged it for Gail's, greedily sucked the air from her tank. His heart was racing, he tried to inhale slowly to slow it.

What was it going to be like when Gail's cylinder was empty? He wished he could be narked, his brain made fuzzy with nitrogen narcosis, before that happened. He'd heard narcosis was pleasant, that divers often hallucinated beautiful images, that they sometimes believed they could breathe water like a fish even as they drowned. But he wasn't deep enough, nor had he been down long enough, for that blessing to occur. So he was glad that at least he'd be alone in his final moments, with nobody to witness the writhing, screaming, cowardly creature he was about to become.

He pressed his knees and his free hand to the wall, tried one last time to pull his arm out of the vise that held it. The pain that shot up his neck from his shoulder made his vision go white and he stopped before he passed out. Under that rock, his forearm was probably mashed potatoes. No, it would probably appear more like overcooked spaghetti, white and limp and covered in blood like tomato sauce.

He'd never imagined dying like this. In a fire or a building collapse, maybe. People would call him a hero then, even if he was merely doing his job. What would people call him after he died in a stupid diving accident while on vacation?

It was so unfair. He'd finally found a woman he wanted to spend the rest of his life with, and then he'd finally screwed up the courage to ask that woman to marry him. It still amazed him that Gail had said yes. Just remembering her face when she'd said it gave him a warm glow inside.

Maybe he was getting narked, after all.

He leaned back to stare at the glittering surface so far overhead. The moon was so beautiful tonight. At least that was something to focus on.

Chapter 35

Gail came to on the dock, with a flashlight blinding one eye. She couldn't see at all out of the other one and raised a hand to it. The blocking object was removed, and Marina stared down at her, and then pressed the bloody napkin back to Gail's brow, partially blocking her vision again. "Lie still, Gail. You have a nasty head wound, and most likely a concussion."

Her throat was dry, her lips were chapped, and she could barely get the question out. "Leon?"

Something heavy thumped down onto the dock at her side, and more faces looked down on her now.

"Leon?" she croaked again.

Marina peered into the distance over the water. "They'll get him, Gail."

Too vague. She couldn't stand it.

"Breathe this, Gail." Marina pressed an oxygen mask over her nose and mouth. The hissing air was cold on her burning face. A shiver passed down her body.

"Leon?" she mumbled through the mask, her voice hoarse.

"Deep breaths," Marina told her, stroking Gail's hair back from her head. "You don't want the bends. And you have a nasty coral rash on your face and hands."

"Leon?" Why wouldn't anyone tell her about him? She tried to sit up, but two pairs of hands pressed her to the dock. The second person was kneeling behind her; she could feel his presence but couldn't see him.

The fourth man she had loved was dead, buried under a

rockslide, drowned in the ocean. Her mind played her personal slideshow of nightmare visions for her. First, Leon, half-buried, floating listlessly in blue-gray water. Terry, a charred corpse, flames still dancing around the driver's seat of his car. Mark, a spread-eagled lifeless mannequin at the bottom of a ravine. Keith, trapped in the smoldering wreckage of his helicopter.

Every single one, her fault. She was the deadly link.

The stars and moon above were mockingly glorious on this tropical night. It wasn't right. It wasn't fair. She shut her eyes to block out all that insulting beauty.

Voices, a mix of Spanish and English, penetrated her consciousness.

"We got him." Diego.

"Stacey's towing him in now."

Tears streaked down Gail's cheeks. They were towing in Leon's body. This was the first time she'd be able to view the remains of her lover before a considerate coroner made the body presentable or prevented her from seeing it at all. Was she strong enough to take this?

"Bring the stretcher. Is the boat ready?"

They'd strap his corpse to the stretcher, take it—she didn't know where. Presumably they had morgues in Honduras, just like in the US.

Marina took her hand off Gail's shoulder and then pulled the oxygen mask from her face. "Sorry; we need this, Gail."

"Did you alert the hospital?" someone asked.

Gail rasped, "I don't need a hospital."

"Maybe not," Marina agreed. "But Leon could use one right now." She rose to her feet, the mask in one hand and the small oxygen tank in the other, and walked out of Gail's sight.

Gail sat up abruptly. This time nobody stopped her. The moon overhead swung in the heavens for a few nauseating seconds before settling back into place. She turned her throbbing head to look behind her. At the other end of the dock, a cluster of people knelt around a wetsuited body.

Leon.

The boards of the dock undulated beneath her. She was too woozy to walk there. Instead, she crawled on her hands and knees.

Someone had peeled his wetsuit down to his waist, or as shredded as it was, maybe the rockslide had done that. Someone had wrapped towels around Leon's left forearm; the cloth was already stained with blood.

His right arm was folded limply across his chest, as if someone had placed it there for the final repose. His skin, where it wasn't bloody, looked blue in the moonlight.

Gail crawled to his head. Leon's face was half-obscured by the oxygen mask. His eyes were closed. Why was nobody doing CPR? Maybe they could bring him back.

Then Leon's eyes opened, and his gaze met hers. Was she hallucinating?

He smiled weakly, and then he looked up at everyone and raised his free hand to give the group a thumbs-up and then the okay sign. Stretching his hand out toward her, he croaked, "Love."

She clasped his cold fingers in hers, leaned forward and held his hand against her cheek.

She couldn't believe it.

Leon was alive.

Chapter 36

Leon's left arm was broken in two places, his shoulder had been dislocated, and he sported a wide variety of cuts and bruises from falling rocks. Gail had a mild concussion, a gash and a bruise on her forehead, and coral rash on her cheeks, neck, and hands. They had to stay an extra two days in Roatan before they were deemed fit to fly home.

"This is proof we belong together," Leon quipped as they relaxed in hammocks on the Coco View dock, unable to dive. "We can survive anything."

The night before they flew back home, Gail abruptly woke up, her heart pounding with alarm. Leon was leaning over her. "Bad dream?"

In the nightmare, she'd been standing at the bottom of a cliff, and Mark's body had just crashed onto the ground at her feet.

"Who is Mark?" Leon quietly asked. "I think that's what you said. Mark!"

She licked her lips and swallowed, then pushed herself up and reached for the water bottle on the bedside table. "You know about Terry. And I told you about Charlie's father, Keith. But I haven't told you about Mark Branderman. We were engaged."

She told him the rest of the sad story.

He pulled her into his side with his uninjured arm and kissed the top of her head. "I'm sorry you've been through so much tragedy, Gail. Nobody deserves that. But you've got me now. I'm not going anywhere, and our future will be happy, I promise you. I can't wait until we're married."

Gail waited until they'd landed in Seattle to tell him. It was impossible to find the right time and place. She finally gave up and chose the luggage carousel as they waited for their suitcases.

"Lion Man." She grasped his good arm. "My dear, sweet, funny Leon."

He placed his hand over hers. "Yes, my amazing, wonderful fiancée?"

"I can't marry you."

She watched his eyes, saw the uncertainty ripple through his thoughts. Then he grinned. "Ha! It's because of number 9, isn't it?" He leaned close. "It was a simple affair, sweetheart. Nine means nothing to me." He waved his hand theatrically in the air. "She's only a crab."

"I'm serious." She focused on his Adam's apple as he swallowed.

"Gail, what the hell?"

"I nearly killed you." She tried to pull her hand away from his.

Frowning, he held on. "What are you talking about? You saved my life."

A young woman on the other side of Leon nudged her male companion, then whispered to him and pointed in their direction.

"That accident never would have happened if it hadn't been for me." Gail inclined her head toward Leon's blue roll-on bag coming down the conveyor belt in their direction.

He let go of her hand to awkwardly snatch the bag one-handed off the carousel, then set it on the ground and turned back to her. "Gail, that's crazy talk."

The young couple were staring at them now, eagerly eavesdropping. Gail shifted her gaze from them to Leon's face.

"Keith. Mark. Terry. Don't you see? I'm the common denominator. It's not my fault, it's not your fault. It's a curse."

"Sweetheart, you're just scared."

"I know it sounds crazy. It *is* crazy. But this is what happens." She had to make him understand. "I'm a serial killer. The men I marry, even the men I *promise* to marry, die."

The young couple moved a few steps away.

Blinking rapidly, Leon stared at the carousel. Her green bag was coming around. Leon grabbed it from the conveyor belt. Setting it down beside her, he reached for her hand again. "I'm not scared, Gail. I can't wait to marry you."

Gail's breath caught in her chest. This hurt almost as much as burying her husband. She swallowed hard. "Leon, I am so honored that you want to marry me. I would love to be your wife." Pulling her hand away, she wrenched off the engagement ring, scraping her rash-swollen knuckle. "But I can't do that to you. I love you too much. We can still date. We can still have fun. But I can't marry you."

His eyes filled with tears, and his jaw briefly tightened. Then he swallowed before saying in a hoarse voice, "You saved my life. Gail, you *are* my life."

She'd never seen such a stricken look on a man's face. Her heart ached at the sight, and she wanted to embrace Leon, but she made herself stay strong. "I won't marry you."

For a long, painful moment, they stared at each other in suspended animation. Then Gail pushed the ring into Leon's pants pocket, and reached for the handle of her roll-on bag.

Grabbing the handle of his own suitcase, Leon turned and quickly strode off into the crowd. She watched him go through a blur of tears.

Charlie arrived from the Cell Phone Waiting Lot only three minutes after Gail called. "Whoa!" she said, seeing the forehead bandage and the coral rash on her mother's face. "What kind of vacation was this?"

"The roller coaster kind." Gail hefted her suitcase into the back and then slid into the passenger seat. "Wonderful, horrible, and now back to real life. I can't wait to see my cat."

Charlie rolled her eyes. "Orion's fine. I kept him in like you asked, and he used the litter box okay. But your bed is getting pretty fuzzy with cat hair. Hey, I heard there was an earthquake in Honduras. That wasn't anywhere close to you, was it?" Charlie peered out the windshield. "Where's Leon?"

"Leon and I are no longer together." Gail massaged her empty ring finger as she cried all the way home.

Chapter 37

When she arrived back at her flower shop in Seattle, Gail was appalled to find the front window covered in plywood. She quickly dialed Candace Fischer, who had subbed for her while she was on vacation.

"I'm so sorry," Candace said on answering. "I didn't want to ruin your vacation, Gail. It happened sometime in the middle of the night, only two days after you left. A vandal, I guess. The police think maybe the window was broken with a tire iron or something like that. Nothing was stolen; I'd already taken all the cash out of the register."

Gail was perplexed. The vandal behind all the destruction at Langston Green had been caught and was currently in jail. There hadn't been any further damage there, and she couldn't fathom why anyone would want to target her flower shop. Her brain flashed back to the night her car mirrors had been smashed. Was someone targeting *her*? "Do the police have any clue who did it?"

"Probably just kids. I found one weird little slip of paper, but it probably blew in from the street through the broken window. It just had a big letter *K* written on it in rust-red ink. The police took it."

K? Karma? That was the name she'd seen on Leon's phone. The name she'd heard in the fire station.

"No threats or anything," Candace summarized. "I cleaned up and had the window boarded up. The police report's in the top drawer under the cash register, along with the bill for the window work. I stayed in the shop for a day after the incident, but not a single customer walked in, so I hung out the closed sign and locked up. You don't have to pay me for the days I didn't work. I would have called the insurance company, but I don't know who you use."

"I'll take care of it. I'm sorry you had to deal with all that." Gail thanked Candace for her diligence and assured her a paycheck was in the mail before hanging up.

She studied the dark shop. The flowers in the cold case looked as if they'd still be saleable for another day or two, and as far as she could tell, nothing else had been damaged. She plucked one of the fairy wands from a vase on the counter, closed her eyes, and waved it in the air. "I wish this hadn't happened. I wish Leon had never proposed. I wish for an easy, happy, safe future."

Naturally, when she opened her eyes, nothing had changed. Real life was not a fairy tale.

Last night, she'd left voicemail and texts for Leon, saying she was devastated for hurting him, and that although she'd retracted her acceptance of his proposal, she still wanted to have a relationship with him.

There'd been no response from him. The guilt kept her up all night, but she kept reminding herself how much worse she'd feel if he died after they were married. Now she at least had the comfort of knowing he was alive and getting on with his life.

Sighing, she reached for the computer to find her insurance records and locate a company that would replace the window.

Chapter 38

"What do you think about Gail's vandalism problem?" Jon Park asked.

"What?" Leon glanced at his partner from the passenger seat as Jon pulled to a stop at a red light. It felt weird to sit on this side of the aid truck, but with his arm still in a sling, he hadn't been cleared to drive. He felt useless in general. With Conrad riding in the back to do the heavy lifting when needed, Leon was only along to dispense advice to his less experienced EMT partner.

"Charlie told me. You don't think that could be Karma, do you? Your Karma?"

"She's not my Karma; she's never been *my* Karma."

"Okay, okay."

Leon rubbed his jaw with his free hand, remembering that he hadn't told anyone except Donovan Kelly and the court clerk about the catnapping. And so far, nobody else knew about the no-contact order he'd filed for, either. "That woman is mentally ill or something. But—vandalism? A note? What are you talking about?"

The light turned green and Jon stepped on the gas. "The broken window at Gail's Flowers. You know, the one that got busted while you two were on vacation. There was a slip of paper with only a letter *K* that looked like it might have been written in blood."

An alarm went off in Leon's head. All the problems Gail had over the last few months suddenly converged in his mind.

The smashed side mirrors on her car. The SLUT sign spray-painted on her garage door. The beheaded rats. The cat. Karma was responsible for everything.

Oh, sweet Jesus, Karma even knew where Gail worked. She knew which car Gail drove. His court hearing for the restraining order was set for next week, and now he truly needed to include Gail Langston's name on it, too, for her own protection. He groaned. "Shit."

"What's wrong, Lion Man?"

"Life. I filed for a no-contact order against Karma. What they call a civil antiharassment order. I filed the paperwork right before we left for Roatan."

"Yeah?"

"The court notified Karma while we were gone. So yes, I'd guess that she broke that window in Gail's shop. I think she was the one who wrote SLUT on Gail's garage door. I know she kidnapped Gail's cat. And she cut the heads off a couple of animals and left the corpses at Gail's, too."

"Cut the heads off what animals?" Jon darted a look at Leon before turning his attention back to the road.

"A couple of rats." He'd have to tell Gail, and the whole world, about this mortifying relationship with a psychopath. "How can I protect Gail if I'm not with her?"

"So Karma threw a fit when she got the notice," Jon said. "I think the window got broken on December 20. Has she done anything since then?"

Leon rubbed his forehead with his free hand. "Not that I know of."

"So maybe you scared her off. Maybe you've already fixed the problem."

"Nice thought, Jon. But I doubt I'll be that lucky."

"Then maybe you should talk to your pal Donovan about the next step. And are you sure you can't still be with Gail?"

Leon grimaced and studied the scenery outside the truck

window. He didn't want to admit that it hurt too much to see Gail Langston if they didn't have a future together. He'd *so* wanted that future. For the first time in his life he could see it, taste what it would be like to share his entire life with a woman. A life partner. With Gail Langston. For the first time, he could envision a happy retirement after he was too old to work for the fire department. He could see the two of them decorating a new house they would purchase together, going on trips together, sharing community projects. He'd laid everything on the line, his whole heart, his whole being. He'd risked his very soul, and she'd made him so happy when she said yes in Roatan. And then . . .

Pounding his fist on the dashboard in frustration, he growled, "Why is my life turning to shit?"

"I've got your back, Leon. But since I'm dispensing advice, can I say that maybe you jumped the gun with Gail? Proposing after what, three months?"

Leon glared at him.

"You really thought it'd stay a secret when Conrad, April, and Stacey were all there?"

Between his problems with Karma and his grand public gesture with Gail, his future looked to be a morass of humiliation, trouble, and sorrow. Leon sighed. "I guess not."

Chapter 39

Although Elisa still wanted to manage the nursery alone, she came up with the brilliant idea to move Gail's flower business to Langston Green. Gail couldn't wait to close Gail's Flowers in Seattle at the end of January when her lease was up and relocate to the family business center. With the addition of the little sculptures and the word-of-mouth and *Seattle Weekly* article about personalized bouquets, business had picked up, but only until the window was broken and boarded up. It had taken another week to get new glass installed, and that closure of the shop seemed to have discouraged any new customers. Meanwhile, down the street, Trader Joe's was still doing its usual booming business; the street continued to host a parade of patrons walking by with inexpensive bouquets tucked into their shopping bags.

With Gail's services moved to Langston Green, the nursery greenhouse could still supply the flowers without the cost of delivering them as they did now, and the new building at Langston Green had room to display all sorts of interesting additions for her personalized bouquets. She could teach classes there on flower arranging, and maybe one on how to transform basic boring glass and ceramic vases into more unique containers. She could help Elisa care for Timo and Rosa, who for now were living with her daughter in Elisa's new living quarters on the second floor of the new building. Jeannie was also willing to teach some painting and crafts classes at the nursery, although she used the word "facilitate," because she said she wasn't really an art teacher.

Gail hadn't heard a single spoken word from Leon after they'd split at the airport. She'd left him text messages asking to meet him somewhere, explaining that she still wanted him in her life. He'd replied with four words: *It hurts too much.*

Then she'd heard nothing more. So now they were apart and both were aching. And although she knew she'd done the only thing she could, her guilt was almost overwhelming, especially during the nights when she had only Orion to comfort her.

She tried to pick up the pieces. Even if she wouldn't have Leon's love and companionship, she could still have a satisfying life. She'd still be Jeannie's friend, and they would continue to make art together. Maybe she could even find a scuba club that didn't include the fire department gang. Seeing Leon's friends would be too embarrassing and painful. She sighed.

She was sketching out some ideas for her section of the Langston Green building when the bell on the shop's front door chimed. The redhead who walked in looked vaguely familiar. And definitely hostile. Her green eyes glittered with malice as she said, "It's all your fault."

Gail was taken aback. "What?"

"What in the hell do I have to do to get you to go away?"

Speechless, Gail stared at her.

"Leo loves me," the woman snarled. "Why are you keeping us apart? Why can't you get it through your head that we don't want you in our lives?"

Gail zeroed in on a memory. This was the woman who had come into the shop once before, boasting about her passionate relationship with an EMT. A. K. Strand. Was the *K* for Karma? The name on Leon's phone. The *K* on the note. "Karma? Are you Karma? Are you talking about Leon?"

"Leo." The redhead smiled as she unzipped her handbag

and reached in. "We both prefer 'Leo.'"

Gail glanced at the desk phone. If only it would ring right now. Could she fake hearing her cell phone from the back room? "Did you break my front window, Karma? Why would you do that?"

"Did you enjoy those rats? I wanted to do your cat, too." The woman smiled menacingly. "But now, since you can't take a hint, I'm going to fix this once and for all." The woman pulled out a pistol and aimed it at Gail.

"What? Why?" Gail's heart leaped into overdrive. "There's no need for this, Karma." She stepped out from behind the counter to have a more personal conversation. "We don't even know each other."

"I know you, all right," Karma spat. "You're the one that's in the way."

The gun went off.

Chapter 40

Leon's cell phone dinged while he and Jon were in the middle of a mass-casualty training exercise with other first responders near Lynnwood. He struggled to complete his triage assignment with only one usable arm, and he was relieved when the exercise was finally deemed a success and all the volunteer "victims" stood up to leave.

Back in the passenger seat of the rig, Leon checked his phone. Even routine tasks like this were awkward, with his left arm still in a cast and sling. The hand and fingers on his mangled arm still worked, thank God.

The text that appeared on his cell phone screen nearly gave him cardiac arrest. It was from Karma. Alice Karmen Strand had given her best performance yesterday during their court hearing, crying crocodile tears as she accused Leon of taking advantage of her drunken state and then leaving her in the lurch when she might be pregnant. She didn't seem to remember that none of that made sense with all the events that she had engineered between them afterward. And after her record revealed that she'd done this previously to another man, the judge had issued Leon his no-contact order. Leon had mentioned the damage Karma had done to Gail's property, but the judge simply said that Gail would have to file for her own order.

After receiving a lecture from the judge, Karma had stomped out of the courtroom, and Leon had hoped that was the last he would see or hear of her. But now the text message on his cell proved that was a futile hope.

I know the bitch is making you do this. I am going to fix it today so we can be together again.

"Oh my God," Leon blurted. "We have to go to Seattle."

"We're supposed to report back to the station." Jon backed the aid truck from the parking spot.

Leon flicked on the siren button. "Just step on it. Hit I-5, *now*!"

"What the hell, Leon?" Jon yelped, his eyes still fixed on the rearview mirror.

"I think Karma is going to kill Gail."

"What—"

"Shut up and drive! Take the Forty-Fifth Street exit to Gail's Flowers." Leon punched in 911 and asked for the Seattle Police.

According to his phone, Karma's message had arrived in his inbox nearly twenty minutes ago. He knew Karma was unstable; he should have foreseen this.

Leon's thoughts swung wildly to various scenarios, from Karma wrecking Gail's shop, breaking vases and tossing flowers into the street, to threatening Gail with a tire iron, or even Karma slitting Gail's throat with a knife, the same way she'd slit his painting.

He prayed that he was not going to arrive too late.

Chapter 41

Gail's leg felt as if it had been whacked with a baseball bat. She staggered backward into the wall. Looking down, she saw the hole in the thigh of her pants leg, a small black spot marring the white fabric. And then the blood spurted out. A hot wetness dripped down the back of her calf, and the pain in her thigh changed to a searing burn. Her leg betrayed her, collapsing. She slid down the wall, feeling the slick dampness of blood behind her. She knew that the front of a bullet wound—the entry point—was much smaller than the exit wound. She had no way of looking at the back of her thigh, and she wasn't sure she wanted to. The growing pool of blood on the floor around her proved that she was bleeding heavily.

This was surreal; everything seemed to be happening in slow motion.

"You made me do that," Karma growled, waving the pistol wildly with one hand as she combed the other through her long red hair.

Gail hoped that the woman might accidentally shoot off her own head, but it didn't happen. Why did good people get killed every day while dangerous nutcases were out running around the streets? The nutcase in front of her took hold of the pistol with both hands again and pointed it at Gail's forehead. "Why did you make me shoot you?"

Gail's head was reeling. Was she dizzy from the loss of blood or the absurdity of the question? She felt nauseous and embarrassed that the seat of her pants was soaked. Blood for sure, but had she wet herself, too? It seemed a ridiculous thought to have right now.

You're not dead yet, she told herself. *Hell, you saved a man from drowning just a couple of weeks ago. Surely you can save yourself now.* She looked around for something, anything, to staunch the flow of blood. Her smock hung from its usual hook on the wall beside her desk. She pointed at it. "Could you hand me that smock, please?"

The woman's eyes narrowed suspiciously. "Why? What are you up to now?"

"Karma," Gail murmured softly. She waited until the other woman's gaze met hers. "I might die unless I can stop this bleeding." They both studied the pool of blood on the tile floor. It had spread to surround Gail's hands. Her fingers looked like bleached starfish in the scarlet liquid.

"You made me do that," Karma repeated. "Why did you take Leo from me? You're the one keeping us apart."

"Leon and I are no longer together."

"Ha!" Karma's green eyes were wild. "You think I don't know that you're behind this court-order stupidity? You think I don't know that you went to the Caribbean with him? You're such a conniving bitch. That was supposed to be *our* honeymoon trip."

Clearly, the smock would not be forthcoming. Gail wiped her hands on the front of her pants and, taking a deep breath, stretched forward and pulled the sneaker from her right foot. She nearly blacked out with the pain before sitting upright again. When the buzzing gnats disappeared from her field of vision, she took another breath, forced her knee to bend, and shoved the sneaker beneath her ruined thigh. Groaning, she lowered her leg onto the shoe and then flopped back against the wall, willing herself not to throw up as waves of pain radiated through her body. She prayed that the pressure from the shoe would make the blood flow stop, or at least slow down. Femoral artery, she remembered. Balling her fist, she shoved it into the crease between her crotch and her leg to apply pressure there. Her entire body already felt cold.

Karma continued to mutter. "You made me do it. You're going to tell Leo that you made me do it."

Gail forced herself to open her eyes and nod. "I will. I know it was an accident."

Karma lowered the gun. "That's right. It's not my fault. I only meant to scare you so you'd leave us alone."

"I understand," Gail murmured. Maybe if she said the right thing, the woman would just leave. Then she could drag herself to the phone. There was still time. Looking up, she tried a shaky smile. "I forgive you, Karma."

The other woman's face changed as swiftly as if she'd been poked with a cattle prod. Taking a step closer, Karma pointed the pistol at Gail's head again. "*You* forgive *me*? *You* forgive *me*?"

She spat out a sound that was probably meant to be a laugh. "*You're* the relationship wrecker. I'm the one who should be forgiving you. But I don't. Leo and I were happy before you came along. You, playing the sad widow. Oh, poor me."

Karma held up a make-believe fiddle with her left arm and stroked the gun across it like a bow. "Black widow is more like it. Poisoning Leo against me."

Gail was getting so cold that she started the shiver. She knew shock was setting in.

"I'm younger," Karma continued. "I'm prettier. I'm a hell of a lot sexier than you. You're just a pathetic old bag of bones."

Gail was afraid to say anything else. The room seemed to be changing dimensions, warping into a parallelogram instead of a proper rectangle. The desk phone rang, but the sound seemed far away. Leon? No, a female voice was speaking;

she'd left the recording on speaker so she could hear it while working on her figurines.

"Hi, Mom," Elisa chirped. "Charlie's here."

Charlie's voice was fainter as she yelled, "Hi, Mom!"

Then Elisa continued. "We're talking about Valentine's Day. We know it's a way off, but we want to run some options by you. And do you want us to invite Leon?" There was a long pause. "Well, guess you have your hands full right now, but we know you'll call back when you can."

Then her daughters chorused together, singing loudly into the phone, "We LOVE you!"

After a click, silence reigned for a few seconds. Then Karma snorted, waggled her head, and bitterly repeated in a loud falsetto voice, "We LOVE you!"

Turning swiftly, Karma fired a shot into the wall above Gail's head, making her jump. Karma's lips were moving, but Gail heard only loud ringing for the space of several dozen galloping heartbeats. When she could finally make out the other woman's voice, it sounded like it was coming from down the block instead of only a few feet away. ". . . have it all, you have everything! You have a family that loves you. Elisa. Charlie. What stupid names!"

Gail wished she could see both her daughters one last time. Charlie and Elisa were as different as daisies and thistles, but they were resourceful and independent. She and Terry had done a great job. Their daughters would be fine. She was sorry she wouldn't be able to see her grandchildren.

"Why can't you let Leo love *me*? I should kill you." Karma pointed the pistol at Gail's forehead again. "That would show him."

Gail was halfway tempted to tell the other woman to pull the trigger. One quick blast might be better than slowly bleeding to death. But either way, she knew Leon would never forgive himself.

Oh God, Leon. She was trembling all over. So cold. All Leon had done was love her, and she'd shoved him away like a groping first date, just because she was scared. He was a good man. He was a kind man. Tender. Passionate. Fun to be with. A rare happy man, at least until she'd crushed his spirit. He took risks only because he wanted to fully experience life. Leon Maxwell had brought her back to life, and she'd punished him for it.

If only she could write him a note. She dipped a finger in the sticky blood and drew a red stripe on her white pants over her good leg.

Karma made no comment, so she dipped her finger again and made a letter L.

The pistol barrel tapped cruelly against her forehead. "What do you think you're doing?" Karma snarled.

O. V.

"Oh, no, you don't; you're not writing a last love letter to him!"

Gail opened her mouth to say, "To my daughters," but then the outside door flew open with a sudden bang.

She'd expected a police officer, or maybe a whole SWAT team, but it was only Leon. Taking in the scene, he swore and then slid to the floor beside Gail. When he pressed a hand on the bullet wound, she nearly passed out.

"Stop it! Stop it!" Karma trained the pistol on Leon now. "You're not with her. You love me!"

Ignoring Karma, Leon ripped off his sling, wadded it into a pad, and pressed it over Gail's leg. "You're going to be okay, sweetheart. Hang in there."

"She is *not* going to be okay," Karma bellowed. "She is going to die! She made me shoot her! And then we are going to be together, Leo, you and me."

Leon stared at the gun pointed at his head. Now Jon Park was standing behind him in the doorway, his mouth open, frozen in place.

"Aren't we going to be together, Leo?" Karma moved the pistol to point at Gail again.

"I'm planning on it, baby." Leon rose slowly to his feet and held out a hand in her direction.

Karma's expression wavered. "But you were trying to save her."

"I'm an EMT." He shrugged. "My training just kicked in."

"She needs to die so we can be together."

Leon took a step closer to Karma. "She is dying. Look at all the blood."

Gail wondered whether he was telling the truth. She closed her eyes. Were those sirens she heard outside? Jon vanished from the doorway.

"It's just you and me, baby," Leon crooned. "I've always loved you."

Gail heard another step.

"I'm a weak man, Karma. But now I know it's you I love. Can you forgive me?"

"Leo, I—"

The gun went off. Gail's eyes flew open. Plaster rained from the ceiling. Karma's pistol was raised overhead. Leon had his right hand on her arm and his broken arm wrapped around her torso, holding Karma tightly in a one-armed bear hug. Two more shots went off as they struggled for the pistol.

"Nooooooo," Karma wailed.

Leon backed the woman toward the counter and with a sudden shove, thrust her into the sharp corner. With a doglike woof, Karma crumpled in pain. Leon wrestled the gun away just as two police officers burst through the doorway, yelling at the top of their lungs. "Police! Gun! Put it down! Put the gun down! Put it down!"

For a few horrible seconds, Gail believed the police might shoot Leon.

"About time you got here." Leon held out the gun, the grip pointed toward the first officer.

After the pistol had been tucked into the officer's belt, the police seemed to grasp who was who and quickly handcuffed Karma and dragged her out of the shop.

Then Leon was back by Gail's side, painfully pressing on her wound and brushing her hair gently away from her forehead. "Hang tight, sweetheart. The ambulance will be here any minute."

"Leon, I . . ." It was hard to get the words out.

She was so cold. So tired. She had to tell him now, just in case.

She shifted her gaze down to her pants leg. *I LOV.* "I wanted to tell you."

His eyes were swimming with tears. "You can tell me anything, Gail."

"I was wrong," she whispered.

He smiled weakly.

No, that wasn't the most important thing she needed to say. "I love you."

"I love you, too."

Two Seattle paramedics left a stretcher at the door and jogged inside.

"I want to spend the rest of my life with you," she told Leon.

He squeezed her fingers. "I want that, too, Gail."

"Will you marry me?" she asked. It came out as a gasp, no louder than a whisper.

But then a paramedic pulled Leon away, and the world dissolved into a blur of needles and swirling motions and sirens. Gail fought to retain consciousness. Had he heard her? Had he responded? The room abruptly went black.

Chapter 42

Three months later Gail was still limping, so Leon carried her to the altar. It wasn't much of a feat, given that the minister stood under a portable arch of spring flowers less than fifty steps from the parking lot. The park was a pretty waterfront location, fronting Lake Washington, and it was a rare sunny, windless afternoon in mid-April. Burgers and hot dogs sizzled on the grill, and more than twenty close friends were in attendance.

Jeannie Caber served as matron of honor in a flower-bedecked wheelchair. Gail's daughters Charlie and Elisa served as bridesmaids, dressed in peasant blouses and long skirts with wreaths of miniature roses in their hair. Their men—Charlie's lover, Jon Park, and Elisa's now fiancé, Jake Street—stood up with Leon. Groomsmen outnumbered the bridesmaids, because Leon had also asked Timo to join him. The Guatemalan teen couldn't stop smiling at the honor and stroking his hands proudly over his very first suit.

Gail's mother gave her away, kissing her on the cheek before retreating to her place in the front row.

As they stood before the minister, Leon held Gail's hands and looked into her eyes. "I've never been a husband before, Gail, so I hope you'll forgive my mistakes. But I vow to be the best husband I can be, because that's what you deserve. Whether the rest of my life lasts five days or fifty years, I want to spend it all with you."

Gail was so overcome that she completely forgot the vows she'd written. Through glittering tears, she said simply, "Leon, I'll never stop loving you."

After the "I do's" were said and the bouquet tossed (Jon Park caught it, causing a gale of guffaws among the fire department attendees), the real festivities began. The firefighters played a competitive volleyball game while the less physical types set up a croquet course and knocked wooden balls through the hoops amid mole holes and much laughter. After retrieving her cane from the car, Gail took a solitary stroll to the water's edge, her eyes squinting against the bright setting sun glinting off the blue lake surface.

She and Terry had often rented a boat here to entertain the best clients from Langston Green on lazy August afternoons. She felt his spirit with her today.

"Are you watching this, Terry?" she murmured to the lapping waves. "Look at our beautiful daughters and all these happy friends. Look at my happy life." Pulling off her bridal coronet, she extracted a white rose from the arrangement. She briefly pressed her lips to it, and then tossed it into the water. "Goodbye, Terry."

"Hey!"

She turned to see Leon striding her way. She pressed her floral headdress back into place and then held out her hand. "Hello, love."

The white rose floated away. Its white petals were now barely visible among the glints of sunlight bouncing off the water.

Leon threaded his fingers through hers and stood beside her, looking out at the lake. "What are you thinking about?"

Turning to her new husband, she smiled. "The future."

If you enjoyed *Again*, please consider writing a
review on any online site.
Reviews really help authors sell books.
Thank you!

Acknowledgments

No writer can produce a good book alone. I owe a big THANK YOU to the following people, who read the drafts of this book and helped to improve the story: astute readers Alison Malfatti and Jeanine Clifford, author Rae Ellen Lee (raeellenlee.com), and ultra-professional editor Karen Brown, who is also bestselling author P. J. Alderman. Thanks are owed also to author Sara Stamey (sarastamey.com) for her help in improving the book description.

Books by Pamela Beason

The *Run for Your Life* Adventure/Suspense Trilogy

RACE WITH DANGER
RACE TO TRUTH
RACE FOR JUSTICE

The Neema Signing Gorilla Mysteries

THE ONLY WITNESS
THE ONLY CLUE
THE ONLY ONE LEFT

The Sam Westin Wilderness Mysteries

ENDANGERED
BEAR BAIT
UNDERCURRENTS
BACKCOUNTRY

Romantic Suspense/Women's Fiction

SHAKEN
AGAIN
CALL OF THE JAGUAR (ebook only)

Nonfiction Ebooks

SO YOU WANT TO BE A PI?
SAVE YOUR MONEY, YOUR SANITY, AND OUR PLANET
TRADITIONAL VS INDIE PUBLISHING: WHAT TO EXPECT

Keep up with Pam by subscribing to her mailing list on
http://pamelabeason.com.

About the Author

Pamela Beason is the author of the Sam Westin Mysteries, the Neema Mysteries, and the Run for Your Life Trilogy, as well as several romantic suspense and nonfiction books. She has received the Daphne du Maurier Award and two Chanticleer Book Reviews Grand Prizes for her writing, in addition to an award from Library Journal and other romance and mystery awards. Pam is a former private investigator who lives in the Pacific Northwest, where she escapes into the wilderness to hike and kayak as often as she can.

http://pamelabeason.com

Made in the USA
Las Vegas, NV
12 July 2021